ALANA'S HERO

BROTHERHOOD PROTECTORS HAWAII
BOOK NINE

ELLE JAMES

TWISTED PAGE INC

ISBN EBOOK: 978-1-62695-682-7

ISBN PAPERBACK: 978-1-62695-987-3

ISBN HARDCOVER: 978-1-62695-706-0

ALANA'S HERO

BROTHERHOOD PROTECTORS
HAWAII BOOK #9

New York Times & USA Today
Bestselling Author

ELLE JAMES

PROLOGUE

"We're here! Can you believe it?" Gina rolled her carry-on into the honeymoon suite at the hotel in Las Cabos, Mexico, and spun it away from her, her eyes dancing with excitement.

Alana Neal gave an exhausted sigh. "Yeah, we're here."

"Oh, come on." Gina grabbed Alana's hands and spun her around like she'd just spun her suitcase. "Don't be such a Debbie Downer. From the way I see it, you dumped that loser, and he's the one who looks like the asshat he's proven to be."

"I'm the one who got dumped, but yes, he's the asshat." She started to kick off the spike heels she'd worn on the airplane from Maui.

"But I look like the poor, pathetic loser who wasn't good enough to keep my groom."

"No way. He wasn't good enough for you. If Vance hadn't gone off with the wedding planner, he'd have cheated on you somewhere down the line after you'd combined your bank accounts or bought a house together. It's much better that you saw his true colors before you said I do." Gina frowned down at Alana's attempt to shed her shoes. "What are you doing?"

"Getting out of these. They're killing me."

"You can't get out of that outfit now. We've got some major celebrating to do." She held onto one of Alana's hands and dragged her toward the door.

"We just got here after a thirteen-hour, red-eye flight. Whose idea was that anyway?" Alana shook her head. "My eyes are bloodshot, I'm physically and emotionally exhausted and in no way ready to party."

Gina dragged Alana toward the door. "You can't let that rat bastard win. You have to hit the ground running and show him you don't give a flying flip that he ran off with the wedding planner as you walked down the aisle."

．　．　．

ALANA SNORTED. "Thanks for the brutal reminder." She had a recurring flashback of standing in the middle of the church aisle with guests looking from the empty space where her groom should have been and back to her. The bride… stiffed at her own wedding. The guests' shocked expressions quickly turning to pity replayed in her mind like a movie film stuck on a cycle of rewind and replay.

While Gina had fallen asleep before take-off from Maui, Alana hadn't slept on the plane from Maui to Honolulu, nor from Honolulu to Los Angeles. And she sure hadn't slept from Los Angeles to Las Cabos.

She wasn't sure how she'd face any of those guests ever again. Alana Neal, the poor bride, whose fiancé ran like a thief escaping with the loot. Granted, most of those guests had been Vance's. Alana's invitees had been a tenth of Vance's, consisting mostly of her girlfriends who were also her bridesmaids.

When the best man had read Vance's note out loud to the guests, Alana had marched back down the aisle, and done the only thing any right-minded, jilted bride would do. She'd grabbed a friend and gone on her pre-paid honeymoon without the groom.

Now that she was in Las Cabos, she wasn't sure she should have come at all. She wasn't in the mood to party, and hanging around another beach town hadn't been her idea of a great place to honeymoon in the first place. Not when she lived on the beautifully lush, tropical island of Maui. Still, Vance had paid for the honeymoon, and Alana had had a non-refundable flight. She was going.

The stubborn anger had faded since, leaving behind a tired woman in the red party dress she'd worn since leaving Maui over thirteen hours ago.

"Isn't it a little early in the afternoon to party?" Alana dug in her heels before Gina got her to the door. "Can't we just sleep for now and think about what we want to do tomorrow?"

Gina dropped Alana's hand and planted a fist on her hip. "And what will you do if we stay in the room? Sit around feeling sorry for yourself? Wallow in self-pity? Grieve for a man you really never loved and who obviously didn't love you?"

Heat filled Alana's cheeks. "Well, yes. I

should be allowed to wallow a little, right? I mean, I *was* jilted. At the altar, no less. Don't I rate a pity party for at least one night?"

"You had it on the plane ride over. It's time to celebrate dodging the bullet, my friend." Gina flung open the door and called out into the hallway, "Gird your loins, Las Cabos. We're going to paint this town as red as my friend's go-to-hell red dress!"

Alana sighed as Gina pulled her through the door and down the hallway to the elevator. "Where to first?"

"I don't know about you," Gina said, "but I'm hungry, and it's best to have food in your stomach before drinking the night away. So, pick your poison. This is an all-inclusive resort, is it not?"

"It is." After so many hours in transit, Alana wasn't hungry. For Gina's sake, she'd nibble on something and go through the motions of "showing Vance" she was better off without him.

Gina hit the buffet with gusto.

Alana chose a few items with little interest and asked for tea.

"Tea?" Gina shook her head. "Girl, have a

beer, drink some wine. Hell, go for whiskey. It's all inclusive."

"I want to pace myself," Alana insisted. "I want to find my way back to my room later and *remember* my victory dance tomorrow."

After a few bites of food and over an hour with her feet on the ground, Alana felt a little better.

Gina leaned back in her chair, sipping on a beer. "Personally, I would've dumped Vance's ass when he didn't bother to fly straight back from New York City when you and Kimo were kidnapped."

"We were rescued before he ever heard about it."

Gina wrinkled her nose. "If he was keeping in touch with you the way a man in love should, he'd have known about it. Instead, he was probably sexting his new boo-thing, Kinsley the wedding planner."

"Do you think he was already dating her at that point?" Alana asked.

"They had to have had something going. He spent so much time with her planning the wedding details."

Alana frowned. "That's partially my fault. I

didn't want a big wedding and didn't want to spend a lot of time planning it."

"Sweetheart, Vance defecting with the wedding planner is not your fault," Gina said. "He's a lying, cheating, dirtbag who didn't deserve you and saved you the trouble of dumping his ass in divorce court."

"You're right." The anger returned, lighting a fire inside Alana. "If you're done with your beer, I have some serious celebrating to do. I want to drink my weight in tequila and find the hottest guy in the bar to dance with. I'm counting on my wingman to get some really great pictures to post on my social media. I want all those wedding guests who gave me pitying glances to know I'm not grieving for one second."

Gina laughed out loud. "Now, that's the Alana I know and love. Let's do this!"

As they left the restaurant, Alana followed the sound of music to one of the resort's bars where a mariachi band had just started playing.

"Come on, let's dance." Gina grabbed Alana's hand and tried to drag her to the dance floor.

"Not yet. I need some lubricant to loosen me up." She headed straight for the bartender and ordered two tequila shots. She handed one to Gina and lifted the other. "Here's to being young and single and not being stuck with one loser schmuck for the rest of your life."

"I'll drink to that." Gina held up her shot glass. "Why settle for one guy when you can sample a smorgasbord of men?"

Alana threw back the tequila shot. The liquor burned a path down her throat, warming her insides. She slapped the empty glass on the bar and demanded, "Another!"

The bartender complied.

After tossing back the second shot of tequila, Alana turned to find two more waiting on the bar.

She grinned at the bartender. "Gracias." Handing one to Gina, she turned her back to the bar, her gaze sweeping the room, a warm glow spreading through her body. "Find me the hottest guy in the place. After this shot, I'll be ready to dance." She tipped the glass up, swallowed the tequila and swayed a little as she placed the glass on the bar.

Gina set hers beside it and glanced around the bar. "What about him?" She nodded toward the man who'd just walked in from the entrance, wearing a tropical shirt, khaki cargo shorts and socks and sandals.

Alana snorted. "I can't with those socks."

Gina nodded. "Right. He's cute, but no. Socks with sandals are an automatic no-go. Next!"

"What about the guy in the white polo shirt and pink shorts?" Alana asked.

"Where?"

"Standing just inside the other entrance." Alana tipped her head toward the man.

Gina's eyes narrowed. "I don't know. He's almost too...pretty."

A moment later, another man entered wearing a pastel purple *guayabera* with navy shorts. He leaned in and kissed the man in pink shorts full on the lips.

"Well, damn," Alana said. "He's taken."

Gina sighed. "Why is it the gay guys are always the prettiest?"

"They know how to shop and wear their clothes." Alana studied the two men. "Do you think they'd let me pose between them for my social media post?"

"Let's save that for your backup plan. You deserve a real fling with a man as interested in you as you are in him." Gina's gaze swept the room as she tapped her chin.

Movement behind the gay couple caught Alana's attention.

Apparently, it caught Gina's as well. She let out a long, low whistle and said, "Now that's a man I could sink my teeth into. As long as his wife or girlfriend doesn't come in after him, we have a winner."

Alana's pulse quickened as she studied the tall, ruggedly handsome man with beautifully broad shoulders and narrow hips. He wore black trousers and a plain white polo shirt that emphasized his dark, short-cropped hair and tightly trimmed beard. Her imagination went right to the thought of how that beard would feel brushing against the inside of her thighs.

She cleared her throat. "I think the tequila is working."

"Well, hell, let's get you a margarita to chase the shots." Gina spun to the bartender. A moment later, she handed the drink to Alana.

Alana raised the drink to her lips and murmured. "He's headed this way."

"I'll just exit stage left and leave you two alone," Gina said. "I'm leaving my margarita with you. Either drink it too or offer it to your next friend with benefits."

"Don't you leave me." Alana started to reach for Gina's hand, but she'd already darted out of range, landing at the far end of the bar, smiling at a man wearing a wife-beater muscle shirt and several layers of gold chains draped around his neck. "Oh, Gina. Be careful."

Incoming hot guy headed straight for the barstool on the other side of Alana.

She spun around, afraid he'd catch her staring far too long.

Once he slid onto the stool, he grinned at the bartender. "*Una margarita, por favor.* Make it a big one. I'm here to celebrate."

Alana, feeling the effects of the tequila, turned toward the man. "Celebrating?"

He nodded.

"Me, too," she said and shoved Gina's untouched margarita toward the guy. "Have one on me."

His brow wrinkled. "Isn't that your friend's drink?"

Alana nodded toward Gina at the other end of the bar. "She left it for me, but I'm not quite up to two-fisted drinking yet."

His eyes narrowed. "How do I know you didn't spike it?"

"I'll drink some to prove it." She lifted the glass, took a big enough swallow and slowly licked the salt from her lip. "Mmm. So good." Who was this woman, sexy-flirting with a complete stranger?

The kind who has been dumped at the altar and needed a good ego-fuck to remind her of her own worth.

"When you put it like that…" He reached for the drink.

Their hands touched, sending a bolt of electricity through Alana despite the numbing tequila.

He raised the glass. "To new beginnings."

"That's right. Out with the old and in with the new." She touched her glass to his and drank. As she lowered the glass, the band started playing a sensuous salsa. The man had all the right looks. So had Vance, though this stranger was bigger, broader and more rugged, not polished. Much better than Vance. One of Vance's negative traits was that he refused to dance. She met and held his gaze. "How do you feel about dancing?"

"I come from Irish stock on my mother's

side. We believe in dancing. If you do it right, it's like making love with your clothes on." He winked.

Heat rose up her chest and down to her groin. "Can you salsa?"

"I've done a little."

She drank a big swallow of her margarita and then held out her hand. "Come on. I'll teach you everything I know and bumble through the rest."

"Now that's an offer I can't refuse." He took her hand and led her out onto the dance floor, twirled her around and stepped right into a sexy, sassy salsa.

Alana's head spun with each twirl. She laughed and danced with the hottest man in the bar, thanking her lucky stars Vance had skipped out on their wedding. He and Kinsley deserved each other. And Alana deserved a great *un*-honeymoon with a man whose name she didn't know, who was hotter than Vance and could dance. The night was definitely shaping up into an epic experience she wouldn't soon forget.

CHAPTER 1

PERSISTENT LIGHT KNIFED through the slits of Chase Flannigan's eyelids, bringing him back to consciousness with a jolt. Pain pounded through his temples, his left cheekbone stung and one of his ribs hurt every time he took a breath.

He opened one eye and immediately closed it. The light was blindingly bright. He couldn't remember the light shining this brightly into his bedroom before. Easing open his eyelid again, he stared up at a ceiling fan with blades in the shape of palm leaves.

What the hell? Must have been a helluva brawl.

Forcing both eyes all the way open, he took in the bright walls of the room, the open window and the sunshine streaming through, and relaxed. Oh, yeah, he wasn't in his room back on Coronado. He was in Cabo San Lucas, celebrating his separation from the US Navy.

No more deployments to hot-as-hell countries. No more commanders demanding more than he was physically able to give. No more enemy forces shooting at him from hidden locations. For the next week, all he had in front of him was sunshine and sandy beaches.

Despite his hangover, a smile curled his lips. *Yeah, this is the life.*

When Chase raised his arm and rested his left hand over his eyes to block the sunlight shining on his face, something cool and hard pressed into his eyelid. Lifting his hand, he glanced at it and found that a bright gold band encircled his ring finger. He never wore rings. Rings were what poor suckers who fell into the marriage trap wore. Too many of his buddies had gone to the dark side of matrimony and now had nagging wives and rugrats climbing their pant legs.

Chase was a diehard, sworn-in-blood bachelor, determined to live his days single, footloose and fancy free. His motto was, *Why settle for one item on the menu when you can sample the whole buffet?* Not that he did it often.

The gold band on his ring finger had to be a joke. Something his buddy, Trevor Anderson, had slipped on his finger when he'd been too drunk to care or remember.

A soft moan sounded in the bed beside him.

Chase sucked in a sharp breath and then rocketed into self-defense mode. He rolled over and straddled the intruder in his bed, pinning slender wrists to the mattress.

Wide blue eyes stared up at him from the flushed face of a beautifully tousled blonde.

Beautiful or not, she was a stranger in his bed. "Who the hell are you, and what are you doing in my bed?"

She struggled to free her hands, her naked body bucking beneath his. "Let go of me before I scream," she demanded.

In her fight to free herself, the sheets shifted lower, exposing bare breasts to the cool, air-conditioned room. The rosy tips knotted into hard little buds.

Chase's groin tightened, his cock stiffening where it rubbed against the soft curls over her sex. He liked the way she felt beneath him, but he still had no memory of why she was there. "I'll let go of you when you tell me who you are and why you're in my room."

"*Your* room? This is *my* room—and you'd better get out before I call the police." She bucked again, the movement making him even harder.

"Not your room, lady, and I'm losing patience." *And control.* If he didn't get some answers soon, he'd embarrass himself with a full-blown hard-on.

Her gaze traveled down his torso to his groin, and she gasped. "You're naked!"

"Darlin', in case you haven't noticed…so are you." He glared down at her and then swept her body with a pointed stare. "I don't remember inviting you into my room last night."

"What are you talking about? I didn't invite you into *my* room." She tugged at her wrists. "Now, get out before I scream the house down." The woman drew in a deep breath.

Before she could let it out in a nail-driving screech sure to split his hungover head in two, Chase sealed her mouth with his.

At first, she stiffened, her lips drawing into a tight line beneath his. When he started to lift his head, she opened her mouth again to let out that scream.

Chase clamped his mouth over hers again

and thrust his tongue between her parted teeth, praying she didn't bite down hard.

He treated her to one of his best kisses, one normally reserved for the fortunate women who made it past the wining and dining—women he ultimately made love to.

By the time he lifted his head, the woman lay still, her eyelids slightly closed, and her lips parted as if waiting for more.

"Now, can we start over?" he whispered, trailing a path of kisses along her jaw to her earlobe. "I'm Chase, and you are?"

"I'm…" she started, her mouth curving into a sweet smile, then *bam*, "…being held hostage!" she yelled at the top of her voice.

He didn't want to do it, but he had to. Quickly as he could, he bent and kissed her again, swallowing the words she was spewing from her luscious, full lips.

When she quieted down, he raised his head slightly. "Look, I'll quit kissing you if you'll quit screaming. I'm not here to rape you. I just want answers."

"You already know why I'm here," she said. "Obviously, you gave me some kind of date-rape drug." Her gaze shot to her nakedness. "Otherwise, I wouldn't be lying in this bed naked with a complete stranger. Please," she said, "let me go. I won't tell anyone, I promise. Just let me go."

"I told you, I'm not going to hurt you," he assured her. "And I don't have to rape the women I make love to. They usually come willingly."

"See?" she said. "You must have given me some kind of drug. I wouldn't have come willingly with a stranger. Oh, my God. Did we… did we…"

"Make love, have sex, get funky?" Chase quipped. He tilted his head toward the waste basket near the nightstand. "Based on the condoms in the trash, I'd say it's a distinct possibility." Straightening to stare down at her again, he said, "I reiterate, I don't rape women. You had to have been a willing participant for there to be more than one condom in there. For the record, there are two."

"Oh, you're disgusting. Please, let me go." She tried again to move her arms.

"I'm going to let go of your wrists, so long as you promise not to slug me." He frowned, wondering if it was a good idea to release her. She could have been the one who'd given him the bruised cheek and rib, and she looked mad enough to do damage to him. Since he was naked, she could really hurt him. "Promise?"

She nodded her head.

He let go of her left wrist.

She brought her hand up to cover her breast.

The sunlight shining through the window glanced off something bright on her ring finger.

"Good God, woman. You're married," Chase exclaimed, appalled that her presence in his bed went against one of his golden rules. *Never bed a married woman.* He leaped off her and the bed and stood a couple of feet away, yanking on a pair of boxer briefs. "I don't know how you got into my room, but *I* don't sleep with married women."

"*Married?*" She glanced at his hand and yanked the sheet up to cover her nakedness. "*I'm* not the married one here. *You* are." She pointed to his ring finger. "You lying bastard. I pity the woman who married you. She has to have shit for brains." Tucking the sheet firmly around her, the woman eased out of the bed. "Where have you put my clothes? Is that your game? Keeping me naked in your room because I can't go running down the hallway in the nude?" She poked a finger at him.

"Well, I have news for you, buddy. I don't care if I have to run naked through town. I'm not staying here. You can't keep me, and as soon as I can, I'm turning you in to the authorities."

Chase lifted a bright red dress off the floor and held it up. "This belong to you?"

"My dress!" She grabbed for the dress and held it against her chest. Then her gaze shot to the dresser where a pair of stilettos had landed. She marched over to the dresser, snatched the shoes into her hand and stared down at the paper beneath them. "What the hell?" She dropped the shoes and grabbed the paper. "No, no, no. It can't be. What the hell did you give me last night?" She shoved the paper into Chase's face and demanded, "Tell me this is some sort of sick joke."

He took the document from her hand and glanced down at the words. They were written in Spanish with the English translation beneath. The paper was thick parchment with fancy scrollwork designs on the border. At the top of the page, it read *Acta de Matrimonio,* and beneath it, in English, were the words, Marriage Certificate.

Chase's heart plunged to the pit of his belly

as he skimmed the Spanish to find the signature scrawled at the bottom of the page: *Chase Flannigan.* Beside his name, in neatly written cursive, was the name *Alana Neal.*

He looked at the ring on his finger and then glanced at her.

She stood with what appeared to be a photograph in her hand, staring down at the image, her face blanching a startling shade of white. Then she looked to him. "We're married?" Her finger pointed from him back to herself, wrapped in the sheet. "You and me? Married?"

With the proof in his hand, Chase had a hard time refuting her statement. He ran his free hand through his hair. "I don't remember signing this."

She looked over his shoulder at the document. "Is that your signature?"

He nodded. "Looks like it." He jabbed his finger at the name Alana Neal. "Is that yours?"

She closed her eyes. "I'm not believing this. It can't be." She spun, dropped the sheet and slipped the dress over her shoulders. "Whatever the hell happened last night...*didn't,* as far as I'm concerned."

"What do you want me to do about this?" He held up the marriage certificate.

"Tear it up. It didn't happen. You and I are *not* married. No way, no how." She snatched her heels off the floor, marched for the door and held it open. "Get out of my room."

He shook his head. "I can't."

"You sure as hell can." She waved her shoes at the hallway. "Go. Now."

"Ms. Neal…Alana…this is my room."

"If this is your room…" Leaving the door open, she marched to the closet and flung open the door. "Why are my clothes in…" Her gaze took in the crisp white, men's shirt and dark trousers hanging neatly beside a pair of jeans and one of the polo shirts his buddy Trevor said he'd need to fit in with the clientele at the all-inclusive resort. "Where the hell is my suitcase?" She ducked her head into the shallow closet as if searching for a hidden compartment. As she straightened, she pressed a hand to her forehead and swayed. "My head feels like steel wool, and I think I'm going to throw up." She pinched the bridge of her nose and glared at him. "What have you done with my things?"

"Listen to me," he said as slowly and as clearly as he could. "This. Is. Not. Your. Room."

"Yes, it is. It says so right on the door. Room 336." She crossed to the door and pointed at the numbers on the door.

"That's 326, not 336." He leaned out the door and jerked his thumb toward the opposite end of the hallway. "Your room is down there."

She frowned, stared at the numbers, blinked and stared again. With a huff, she whirled and searched the room, her gaze landing on the dresser in his room. "If this isn't my room, is that my room key?"

Chase retrieved the keycard from the dresser and ran it over the door's locking mechanism. The light turned red. He tried again. The light blinked red. "I guess, it is."

She snatched the key from him and marched down the hallway, muttering, "I'm not married. I didn't come to Cabo to get married. This is not happening. It's all one horrible, horrible nightmare. *Gina!*"

The woman was spitting fire, and Chase found it strangely charming. The marriage certificate still in his hand, he followed, telling himself he wasn't interested, but needed to resolve this little matter of their marriage. "This appears to be a legally binding document. We can't just tear it up," he called out after her.

As much as Chase abhorred the institution of marriage, he kind of liked torturing Alana with the idea she might be legally bound to him in holy matrimony. This thought gave him an inordinate amount of pleasure. He followed her to room 336. "We can't just tear up this certificate. It's stamped, and a copy is probably stored in some archive somewhere."

"We sure as hell can," she called over her shoulder. "What happens in these kinds of places stays in these places. That certificate won't hold up in the US courts. I'm a US citizen, subject to the US court system. I'm not married." She waved her keycard over the door lock, and the light turned green. Alana pushed into the suite. "Gina!" Without waiting for a response, she charged across the room like a bull toward a matador's red cape and flung open a door. "Gina! What the hell happened last night?"

A startled squeal sounded from the bed. "Geez, woman. Haven't you ever heard of knocking?"

CHAPTER 2

ALANA DIDN'T GIVE a rat's ass about protocol. This was an emergency. But then she blinked.

Gina lay in bed in the arms of yet another stranger.

The man was broad-shouldered, had tattoos on his biceps, shaggy blond hair and a week-old beard that looked devilishly good on him.

Not that Alana cared. "You were supposed to have my back last night. What happened?"

Gina grinned and pointed to a spot over Alana's right shoulder. "Him."

Alana turned to find Chase standing at the threshold of the bedroom door, a frown pulling his eyebrows together over his nose and still not wearing anything but boxer briefs. Then his frown cleared, and he waved a hand in the direction of the bed. "Hey, long time no see."

Alana stared from Chase to Gina and back. "Gina, you know this man?"

Gina shook her head. "Nope, but I wouldn't mind getting to know him."

The man lying in the bed beside her tweaked the tip of her nipple through the sheet. "Sweetheart, you better not know him. I'm not much into sharing my women."

"Carson, I thought you were in Mexico, but I wasn't sure where." Chase grinned. "What's it been? Three months since your separation from the military?"

"Make that four, but it feels like a lifetime." The man in the bed sat up, taking the sheet with him.

Gina squealed and grabbed for the sheet to cover her naked form.

"How's it going, Flannigan?" The man in the bed flung the sheet aside and stood in all his butt-naked glory. He stuck out his hand to Alana. "Carson Walsh."

When she pulled back, Chase grinned, shook the man's hand, and then pulled him into a bear hug. "Glad to know you're still alive and kicking." He pounded Gina's bedpartner on the back.

"It's good to see you, man," Carson said. "You're a sight for sore eyes. How are things with our old Navy SEAL team?"

"I don't know," Chase said. "I'm out on terminal leave."

ALANA SHOOK HER HEAD. "There's nothing unusual about two naked or nearly naked strangers standing in my hotel suite, hugging and patting each other's backs like long lost friends. "I don't believe this. I don't freakin' believe this." She held up her left hand to Gina and pointed at her ring finger. "Did you know about this?"

Gina blinked, and her eyes widened. "What the hell?"

"Exactly what I said." Alana paced the short length of the room in her bare feet and red dress. "Married." She jerked her head toward Chase. "Show her the evidence."

He held up the marriage certificate. "Signed and sealed." He frowned. "And neither one of us remembers any of last night."

"Nothing?" Gina asked. "Not even dancing in the bar downstairs?"

"Nothing," Alana said. "Zero, nada." She moaned as a stabbing pain split her head in two. She pressed her palms to her temples. "I have one hell of a hangover to prove it."

"Oh, honey," Gina said. "This is too rich." A chuckle sounded from deep in her throat. Then it turned into laughter, and soon, she was slapping her hand on the mattress, her eyes streaming with tears of mirth. "Oh my God, this is too funny."

Alana stopped in the middle of her pacing and glared at her friend. "Are you kidding me? You're laughing when I'm married to a man I've never met?"

Gina wiped the tears from her eyes. "You have to see the irony."

"I don't see anything other than an annulment in the very near future." Alana stalked out of the room. "As soon as I've had a shower and a change of clothes, I'll see that this mess is undone."

She stomped into the other room and found her suitcase on the floor where she'd left it when they'd arrived the evening before. Neither one of them had bothered to unpack.

They'd headed straight down to the bar to celebrate her near miss with matrimony.

Alana groaned. *Near miss, hell. Near miss in the States and, the next day, a direct hit in Mexico.*

"Perhaps, you can tell us what happened last night," Chase said from the doorway of the other room.

Gina chuckled. "Obviously, you two got drunk. I only know what happened at the bar in this hotel." Her voice grew closer as Gina moved from her room into Alana's. "Alana wanted to start the party as soon as we arrived, so we went down to the bar."

"Me?" Alana snorted. "You practically dragged me out of the room before I could even unpack."

"You...me...whatever." Gina shrugged. "The point is, there was a band playing, and Alana downed three tequila shots to get the ball rolling. Within an hour, she added two margaritas to the total," Gina patted Alana's back. "Sweetheart, you were pretty happy by the time this guy showed up." She tilted her head toward Chase. "Then you two started dancing salsa, which wasn't half bad." Holding the sheet up with one hand, Gina held out her other hand.

"By the way, I'm Gina. Nice to meet you. I'm Alana's best friend."

Alana snorted. "Best friends keep best friends from doing stupid stuff."

"Chase Flannigan," Chase said and shook hands with Gina. "Nice to meet you, too."

"Don't go getting chummy with this devil," Alana said as she dragged her heavy case up onto the bed, unzipped and opened it.

Inside were layers of frothy lace and the sheer fabric of sexy lingerie. She rifled through the contents, tossing see-through nighties onto the floor. "Where are my clothes?"

Gina pressed her fingers to her lips and gave a sheepish grimace. "The bridesmaids took them out. Each of us put one sexy nightie in their place."

Alana turned on Gina, glaring. "Are you telling me I don't have any other clothes than what I arrived in?"

Gina gave her a weak shoulder shrug. "We didn't think you'd leave your room. There are enough sexy night gowns in there for an entire week." She grinned. "We thought you'd be happy. I mean, who leaves their room on their honeymoon?"

"Honeymoon?" Chase stood in the doorway, his hands planted on his hips. "You're here on your honeymoon, and you ended up marrying me? That's…that's bigamy."

Alana tossed a deep red teddy nightgown over her shoulder. "I'm not a bigamist. I didn't marry the bastard."

"He ran off with the wedding planner," Gina said.

"Gina!" Alana squealed. "No one else had to know that little bit of information but you and me."

Her friend snorted. "And everyone who showed up for the wedding. If you ask me, you dodged a fifty-caliber bullet."

"I didn't ask you, and I'd appreciate it if you kept your Army analogies about my personal life to yourself." Alana threw a sheer black froth of a babydoll nightgown at Gina. She missed, and Chase caught it before it hit the ground.

His brows lifted. "Let me get this straight… You're here on your honeymoon, without the groom, and this is all you have to wear besides that red dress?" He held the black nightie by his index finger, a grin spreading across his face.

Alana tossed more items out of the suitcase, torn between anger and defeat. "It appears I'm wearing the extent of my street clothes, besides a thong bikini." She glared across at Gina. "You owe me."

"I can loan you a pair of shorts and a couple of T-shirts," Gina said, wincing.

Alana threw her hands in the air. "Great, at least I won't have to run to the store in my evening attire."

"I wouldn't toss the lingerie too soon," Gina warned. "You might yet have use for it." She winked at Chase. "I mean, seriously, these weren't cheap." She touched a finger to the sheer fabric.

"Wow." Carson appeared in the doorway, dressed in jeans and pulling a shirt over his head. "Where was that last night?" he asked Gina.

"In Alana's suitcase," Gina said. "That's the one I bought for her wedding trousseau." Gina took the garment from Chase and held it to her chest, fumbling to keep the sheet from dropping. "You might be happy to know, I bought one just like it in royal blue for myself."

"*R-r-r-rrr,*" Carson said, rolling the Rs across his tongue. He grabbed Gina from behind and kissed her neck. "I'm going for coffee. You want any?" He nuzzled the curve of her shoulder.

Gina giggled. "That tickles." She turned in Carson's arms. "Make mine a caramel latte."

"You got it." Carson turned to the others in the room. "Anything for you, Alana, Flannigan?"

"I'm not Alana Flannigan. I did not marry this man."

"That's not what I meant." Carson's lips twisted. "Alana, do you want anything?"

"Yeah." Alana jerked her head toward Chase. "Take him with you, will ya?"

"Wanna go?" Carson asked, his eyebrows rising.

Chase shook his head. "No, thanks. I'm heading down to find breakfast, after I shower and change."

A cellphone chimed from Gina's bedroom. She frowned and disappeared into the room.

Alana turned to face Chase. "Why are you still here?"

"I'm just leaving." He spun on his bare heels and started for the door.

Gina called out, "Holy hell, Alana. You and Chase have to see this."

Alana frowned. Gina tended toward drama. "What is it, now?"

"I got a text...from *your* phone number." She entered Alana's room, her face pale. "It's not good."

Alana's frown deepened. "What do you mean?"

"Look at this." Gina shoved her cellphone into Alana's hand.

Alana glanced down.

UNKNOWN: Tell Alana her husband better meet me behind *La Casa Loca* at midnight, or I kill the bitch.

"What the hell?" Her picture was at the top of the screen with her name beneath it. "That's from my cellphone?" She shoved Gina's phone at her and searched the room for hers.

"Let me see." Chase bent over Gina's cellphone and frowned. "Son of a bitch."

"Where the hell is my phone?" Alana cried. When her search came up empty, she darted out the door and back down the hallway to Chase's room.

He'd left the door open.

Alana pushed through and searched every corner of his room, but to no avail. She left his room and marched back to hers, meeting

Chase at the door. "Who the hell has my phone?"

Chase shook his head and stepped out of her way. "I don't know. If you recall, we're both having challenges remembering what happened last night."

"I have no clothes. I have no phone." She flung her hands in the air. "And I thought this honeymoon couldn't get worse." She turned all of her anger on Chase and pointed to the door. "You. Man. Get out of my room."

He stood with his arms crossed over his bare chest. "Can't."

"What do you mean, *can't?*"

"You heard the threat. If I don't show up at midnight, he's going to hurt you. What's to keep him from hurting you before that?"

"He has my phone, not my name or address." Alana pointed to the door. "He's not going to find me."

"Cabo San Lucas isn't all that big. If he's a local, he may have ways to find you. And if he does, I *will* be around to protect you. I don't know why he wants a piece of me, but until I figure it out, you're stuck with me."

Gina snorted and laughed all at once. Then she clapped a hand over her mouth. "This is too funny. You came to Mexico to get away from your wedding and landed smack dab in another. The first groom ran off, and now you can't get rid of this one. That's rich." She dissolved into a fit of giggling.

Alana glared at her friend. "You're not helping." Her gaze shifted to Chase. "And you need to get out of here."

He crossed his arms over his naked chest, but his stern look lost some of its starch when his lips twitched. "Not without my bride."

CHAPTER 3

CHASE WASN'T sure if the threat was real or not. Until he knew for certain, he refused to leave this woman, who appeared to be his wife, unprotected. "Look, I'm not trying to be mean, but we're in a foreign country. Even the tourist traps have issues with gang violence. Besides that, drug cartels are out there, and they play for keeps. If this guy is part of a cartel, you could be in serious danger."

Alana planted her hands on her hips. "And you're a complete stranger. How do I know you're not just as dangerous as a cartel thug?"

"The US government granted me a Top Secret clearance. If they can trust me, why can't you?"

Alana shot him a pointed glare. "If you really are a Navy SEAL—and I have no proof that you are—you could be nothing more than a trained assassin. Top Secret probably just means you can't kill and tell."

"Ahhh. You two are too stinkin' cute," Gina said. "You're having your very first fight as a married couple."

Alana flung her hands in the air. "We're not married!"

Chase waved the marriage certificate. "I have a piece of paper, and we have wedding rings to prove it."

"That certificate is not worth the paper it's written on." Alana turned back to her room. "Even if it were, just because we're married doesn't mean you can boss me around. You can't make me go with you."

"Okay. You don't have to come with me." He turned and marched down the hallway to his room, grabbed his duffel bag, shoved his hanging clothes and shaving kit inside and marched back to Alana's room.

The door was closed. Chase knocked.

After a long moment, Gina opened the door. She took one look at him and grinned.

"Alana, your husband's here," she sang out. Gina leaned close to Chase. "Alana's not normally so…you know…"

"Bitchy?" he finished for her.

"I was going to say *obstinate*, but bitchy works." Gina glanced over her shoulder. "She's had a rough couple of days."

"Yeah? Well, based on that text, it might get rougher." He pushed past Gina. "Since she refuses to come with me, I'm moving in."

"Oh, no, you're not." Alana crossed the room, lifted the phone and dialed the operator. "Give me security." She paused and then spoke into the phone. "Hi, this is Alana Neal in room 336. There's an uninvited man in my room. Please come escort him out." She frowned. "No need to congratulate me. I'm *not* married." She paused, her frown deepening. "What do you mean, half the hotel staff were invited and danced at my wedding on the beach? I'm not married!" She held the phone away from her ear and stared at it as if it had grown horns. "You want to know the name of the man in my room? Isn't it enough that he wasn't invited?" She huffed. "Fine. His name is Chase Flanni-gan… No, he's not my husband. I'm not married. Oh, for the love of—" Alana slammed the phone down and glared at Chase.

"I take it the staff of the hotel witnessed our wedding." Chase couldn't stop the grin spreading across his cheeks.

The look of horror on Alana's face was priceless.

Chase kept his expression bland. "Why don't you accept that we got married last night, and let's retrace our steps to find out what exactly happened. Then, maybe, we can figure out who the hell I pissed off to the point he'll hurt you to get to me." He raised his hand. "Before you tell me to go to hell, I promise to do something to annul our marriage as soon as we get past the danger."

Gina leaned her shoulder against the door to her bedroom and hiked the sheet up higher over her breasts. "You have to give the guy the benefit of the doubt. He's in this mess as deep as you are."

"Why are you sticking up for him? You're *my* friend, not *his*." Alana rolled her eyes and huffed out a breath. "And I don't have to give him the benefit of a doubt. We aren't married. The texting dude isn't going to find me, and I couldn't care less if he finds Navy dude. Maybe it'll be good if the texting guy finds him, then maybe he can knock some sense into his thick skull."

"Oh, sweetie," Gina said, "Text Dude could be part of a gang or a cartel. Like Chase said, they play for keeps. And they don't play fair. Do you really want to see this fine specimen of male hunkiness peppered with bullets and left to die in some Cabo back alley?" she asked, her gaze hungrily raking over the man's naked chest.

Chase grimaced. "That's pretty graphic. But thanks for caring." He raised his eyebrows and turned on a glowing smile. "Come on, Mrs. Flannigan, you haven't even given our marriage a chance."

Alana covered her ears with her hands. "Stop. Just stop." She took a deep breath. "I came to Cabo to relax and de-stress from the fiasco of being jilted at the freakin' altar. I'm more stressed now than when I found out my fiancé punched out with the wedding planner."

"Then help me reconstruct last night, so we can get to the bottom of what happened and, maybe, get a step ahead of whoever is threatening us." Chase took her left hand. "Then we can work on undoing this wedding that neither of us can remember. And, believe me, if I'd been in my right mind, I wouldn't have married you." As soon as the words came out of his mouth, Chase wished he could take them back.

Her chin tilted defiantly, though her eyes widened, filling with tears, and her bottom lip trembled. "Am I so awful that every man who thinks about marrying me wants out before the marriage even has a chance?"

"Now, you've gone and done it." Gina slipped an arm around Alana's shoulders. "Honey, you're an amazing woman. One of these days, an amazing man is going to realize it. Until then, you might not have met the right one."

Alana sniffed. "Might not? I'd say I'm batting a thousand on bad choices."

Chase frowned. Her words cut more than he cared to admit. "Hey, groom, here."

Gina nodded. "That's right. The jury's still out on your groom. Although he might be the one, if you give him a chance."

"Seriously?" Alana stared at her friend as if she'd lost her mind. "I don't know him from a serial killer. How could he be the one? And it's not like we'll be here more than a week. You can't get to know anyone that well in a week."

Gina held up her cellphone. "All I'm saying is that he didn't ditch you when that text came in."

Chase nodded. "What Gina said. I don't run out on my responsibilities." Not that he needed someone to vouch for him. His reputation stood on its own. Well, for those who knew him.

"So, now I'm a responsibility?" Alana sighed. "Fine. I'll help you retrace our steps. The sooner we get to the bottom of this mess, the sooner we can undo the damage and annul this marriage."

"Good, because I don't like being married any more than you do. I'm a confirmed bachelor—and damned proud of it. No offense."

"Correction." Gina pointed to his left hand and the ring on his finger. "You *were* a confirmed bachelor. You've destroyed your record with that marriage certificate."

Chase frowned. "As I said, we'll work on annulling the marriage as soon as we're past the danger."

"As long as you didn't consummate the

union." Gina's eyes narrowed. "You haven't had sex, have you?" Her gaze shot to Alana.

Alana's cheeks glowed a bright red.

Gina's grin returned, spreading from cheek to cheek. "You did the nasty?" She raised her hand for a high-five. "Good for you! That will show Vanishing Vance he's not all that important. He can keep his ho-bag wedding planner, and you can raise him a much better-looking Navy SEAL."

Alana ignored Gina's high-five and shook her head. "My life isn't a competition with my ex-fiancé."

Gina dropped her hand. "Yeah, but if it were, you'd be winning." She waved a hand toward Chase. "I mean, seriously. He's hot. Look at all those muscles."

Chase tipped his head toward Gina. "Thanks."

Gina's smile tipped slyly. "So, how was the sex? I bet he's even better in bed than Vanishing Vance."

"Gina!" Alana grabbed a pillow from her bed and slung it at her friend.

Gina caught the pillow in one hand, held her sheet up with the other and laughed.

"Did she mention neither one of us can

remember anything that happened last night?" Chase reminded her.

Gina's eyebrows rose. "Dang. You had it going for you until that. If she can't remember the sex, it must not have been that good."

Chase crossed his arms over his chest, ready to defend his ego. "Oh, it was good."

Gina cocked an eyebrow. "How do you know, if you don't remember?"

"I know how to please a woman. If we had sex—and based on the expended condoms in the wastebasket, we did—then it definitely was good. I know how to please a woman."

"Cocky much?" Alana interjected.

"Nope." He puffed out his chest. "Confident. I've never had any complaints."

"But I can't remember last night. That must mean something," Alana pointed out.

"It means we drank some killer tequila," Chase said. "If you want a repeat performance while we're both sober, I'll happily demonstrate." He stepped toward her.

Alana's face reddened, and she raised her hand. "That won't be necessary. I'll take your word for it."

Chase chuckled. "Let me know when you'd like physical proof. I'd be glad to oblige."

"Not happening," Alana insisted.

Gina raised her hand. "I'll take a sample." She waggled her eyebrows and grinned.

"Geez, Gina. Didn't you get enough with Carson last night?" Alana shook her head. "Chase is a married man."

"Not according to you," Gina pointed out.

"Sorry, Gina. I would never cheat on my wife," Chase said. "My mama taught me better."

Gina shrugged. "Didn't hurt to ask."

"Gina, I'll take you up on those shorts and a shirt," Alana said. "I can't go around Cabo in evening attire."

"Coming right up." Gina ducked into her room.

Chase glanced around the suite, consisting of two bedrooms and a sitting room with a red leather couch and two armchairs.

"Where do you want me to put my stuff?" He drew in a deep breath and let it out. "And don't say *where the sun doesn't shine*. I'm staying until the danger is past. If you don't want me to sleep with you, I can sleep on the couch. But I'd prefer to ditch my bag in your room, if you don't mind."

Alana's eyes narrowed, and she seemed to chew on her words before she answered. "Fine.

Put the bag in my room. And no, you're not sleeping with me."

He nodded his head. "Although, since we've already consummated our marriage—"

She frowned and huffed out, "We're not married."

At least she didn't yell that time. Chase grinned. Maybe she was getting used to the idea.

His smile faded. Not that he was interested in continuing the insanity of married life, but he could be worse off. Alana was a pretty blonde. And he must have seen something in her last night to have gone so far as to marry her. His curiosity piqued, he vowed to discover what it was that had pushed him into agreeing to marry her when he'd been shit-faced drunk.

He opened his duffel bag and pulled out his dark trousers and one of the polo shirts Trevor had insisted he needed to wear in Cabo. Chase preferred a T-shirt or a cotton button-up, but the polo shirt might be better for daytime investigations.

He walked to Alana's room and knocked on the doorframe. "Mind if I use the bathroom to shower and change?"

She closed her eyes and shook her head. "Would it matter if I did?"

He cocked an eyebrow. "I could ask to use Gina's?"

Alana inhaled and let go of a long, steadying breath. "No. You can use mine after I shower."

"Thanks. Let me know when you're done. I'll need to let my buddy know I've switched rooms."

"What buddy?"

"Trevor Anderson, another former Navy SEAL. He might come in handy if Text Dude decides to get physical."

"Don't forget Carson," Gina said from the other bedroom. "Three Navy SEALs ought to be able to put the hurt on one cartel thug."

"I'm not worried about one cartel thug," Chase said. "I'm more concerned about a gang of them."

The musical sound of a text message reminder jingled from Gina's room.

Chase stiffened.

"Uh, Mags and Chase…" Gina emerged from her room, carrying shorts and a shirt in one hand and staring down at her smartphone screen in the other. "Text Dude isn't happy that we haven't responded in an hour."

Alana set her suitcase full of lingerie on the floor and crossed to where Gina stood. "What did he say?"

Gina handed her the phone.

I know where your friend is staying.

If she wants to live, her husband better show.

"Alana, this problem isn't going away. He knows where you are." Gina hugged her friend. "Thankfully, your husband is here to save the day." She gave Chase a chin lift. "Get to saving, Frogman."

"All joking aside, I'm on it." He captured Alana's gaze. "You're up first in the shower."

"Trust me, I won't be long. The sooner we resolve this mess, the better." Alana grabbed the shorts and shirt Gina provided and ran for the shower.

Chase didn't like that the threat knew where they were. They'd have to employ escape-and-evasion techniques to stay one step ahead of their predator. If Chase were the only one involved, he'd circle back and confront his aggressor, but he had a wife to consider.

Wife.

Holy hell, what had happened last night that he'd chucked his vow to remain a bachelor and committed to embrace an entirely different set of vows?

ALANA CLOSED the bathroom door and quickly shed her dress, hanging it on the back of the door. Considering it was her only decent outfit for the duration of her stay in Cabo, she had to make sure it remained clean and unwrinkled. She hadn't asked and cringed to think about it, but she hadn't located her panties in Chase's bedroom. Hell, maybe he was the creepy type and kept a pair of underwear from every woman he slept with. A kind of trophy. Sheesh, what had she been thinking last night?

In the shower, she squirted a handful of shampoo into her hand, the shiny ring on her finger giving her pause.

How in the hell had she ended up marrying a man she'd only just met? She'd heard that Mexican tequila was potent, but damn. Somebody must have spiked her drink. And Chase seemed as surprised as she'd been. Could it be his drink had been laced with the same crazy drug as well?

If she could believe him. After being

ditched at the altar by Vanishing Vance, she wasn't sure she could trust any man.

Then why had she trusted Chase enough to marry him last night?

She scrubbed her hair, as if by doing so, she could scrub the man, the marriage and the texting threat out of existence. Unfortunately, the situation wouldn't be that easy to resolve. She rinsed her hair, cleaned her body, the hot water soothing some of the tension in her shoulders.

Gina was right about one thing. Chase Flannigan was hot. If Alana were interested in a relationship, she might go for a man like him. The fact was that she wasn't interested in starting something new. Not now. It didn't seem right that two days before, she'd been happily preparing for her wedding to another man—a man her father had approved of. That should have been her first warning.

All the wedding decisions had fallen on Vance as Alana had been too busy with her job to take the time to pick out napkin colors, cake flavors, florals and the millions of other things her fiancé had wanted in their wedding. Vance had let her choose the place for the honeymoon, and she'd made all those arrangements.

Alana had laid out all of the plans for their lives together. First the marriage, then the honeymoon, followed by house hunting and settling into married life with children in the near future. At the ripe old age of twenty-eight, Alana was finally ready to settle down. Marriage was the next step. Hell, all her friends, except Gina, had been married for years and had one or two children by now. She felt as if her biological clock was like a time bomb ready to blow up in her face if she didn't get on with her adult life.

Looking back, perhaps she'd pushed too hard for that picture-perfect life. She thought she'd loved Vance. But other than being embarrassed and pissed off, she wasn't disappointed the wedding had been called off. She was more disappointed that she wasn't getting on with her plan to be married with children before she turned thirty.

On the flight down to Mexico, she'd realized she'd set herself up for the collapse. The big three-O was going to happen with or without a husband and children. Why was she so afraid of it? God, she'd almost married the wrong man just to put a check in the boxes of "married" and "children." Not only would she have been miserable with Vance, but he would also have been miserable with her. She should thank the wedding planner for taking him.

Then why had she turned around and married the first man she'd met in Mexico? It made absolutely no sense. Had she seen something in Chase she hadn't found in Vance?

Chase was a lot better looking, in a rugged, manly-man way. He was more muscular, taller and stronger. He'd held her pinned to the bed. No matter how she'd fought, she hadn't been able to break free of his grip. Vance couldn't have done that as easily. Thinking of Chase straddling her, holding her wrists tight in his, while his naked body was pressed against her naked body, sent a shiver of lust through her still. Though she wouldn't admit it to anyone, Chase was hung a helluva lot better than Vance. He'd please her much more in bed than Vance ever had. Sex with Vance had been, at best, mediocre.

Now that she knew Chase hadn't been attacking her, she could appreciate his…uh… well…package. Her body heated at the memory. It was a shame she couldn't remember their lovemaking. She ran her hand down her torso to the juncture of her thighs and touched that little strip of nerve-packed flesh. Was it her imagination, or was she a little sensitive down there? She fingered herself, and her breath caught.

Oh, yes. She was sensitive. Drawing her finger down lower to the entrance of her channel, she poked a finger inside. There, too, she was a little more sensitive than usual. The condoms in the wastebasket were pretty damning proof they'd had sex. Her sensitive girly parts only evidenced what she'd thought impossible.

She'd had sex with Chase. Not once, but twice. And she couldn't remember a thing. Her curiosity made her wish she could. The only saving grace to her lack of memory was his total lack of the same memory.

While she was down there, she swirled two fingers inside her channel and then dragged her finger up to her clit. A jolt of sensation made her moan softly. As soon as the sound left her mouth, she clapped her other hand over her lips. But she couldn't stop what she'd started—and she didn't want to. Slowly circling that nubbin of desire, she closed her eyes and embraced the feelings building inside.

As the intensity increased, she stroked

faster and faster until the tingling started at her core and spread outward to the very tips of her fingers and toes. She rode the wave all the way to the end. By the time the tingles dissipated and she returned to sanity, her breathing came in ragged gasps, and her knees shook. She turned her face into the warm spray of the shower and let the water run over her breasts and down to her sex, adding to her overall satisfaction.

She turned off the water and stepped out of the shower, a little cockier and more self-assured than when she'd stepped in. "Take that, Chase Flannigan. I don't need no stinkin' man to get me off." She toweled dry and dressed in the shorts and shirt Gina had provided. The shorts were shorter than she preferred, and the top hugged her breasts a little too tightly, but she couldn't complain. At least it was better than wearing her red dress throughout another day and night. Alana slipped her feet into a pair of flip-flops, the only other pair of shoes she'd found in her suitcase. Tossing her hair up into a turban, she left the bathroom, a smile on her face.

"It's all yours," she said as she emerged from the bedroom with her brush.

Chase's wicked smile took some of the wind out of Alana's sails. "Just so you know, there's barely any sound insulation between the bathroom walls and the bedroom." He leaned close to her as she passed. "You might not need me to get you off, but I promise, I'd make you moan a lot louder."

Fire filled her cheeks. "You did not…"

"Oh, yes, we did," Gina sang from the sitting room. "Quite the entertainment."

Chase's chuckles followed him all the way into the bathroom. Even after he closed the door, his soft laughter could be heard.

Alana glared at Gina. "Why didn't you tell me?"

Gina laughed and held up her hands. "I wouldn't dare come between you and your personal pleasuring, and I hope you'd do the same for me. Besides, I was turned on. And based on the tent in the shorts he put on, so was Chase."

Covering her face with her hands, Alana groaned. "This day couldn't get worse."

"Be careful," Gina warned. "You might jinx yourself. Remember, you have a bad guy gunning for you."

"Oh, Gina, don't be so melodramatic."

Gina's smile faded. "Honey, I hope it's melodrama. I don't want you to be hurt. We've come too far together for me to lose you now."

Alana hugged her friend. "I don't know what I would've done if you hadn't gotten me out of that church before my father arrived. And I certainly wouldn't have come here if you hadn't come with me."

"I love you, sweetie," Gina said. "You're the sister I never had." She pushed Alana to arm's length and touched her cheek. "I'm just glad you didn't marry that spineless piece of shit, Vance. He didn't deserve you."

"I'm glad, too." Alana grimaced. "I think I was so caught up in the whole promise of getting to my happily-ever-after that I never stopped to consider he wasn't the right guy to get me there."

Gina tilted her head toward the bathroom where Chase was singing some song at the top of his voice with words like *something dumb to do* and *want to marry you.* "While you're out retracing your steps from last night, keep an open mind. Even drunk, you wouldn't have married Chase if you hadn't seen something in him worth marrying."

"People do stupid things when they're

inebriated, Gina. Don't read more into the situation than that." Alana pulled the turban off her head and ran the brush through her hair, smoothing the tangles.

"He has a decent singing voice," Gina said. "You have to give him that."

Alana didn't respond to her friend's comment. She didn't have to give Chase anything. They weren't married.

Gina disappeared into her room, muttering something about getting dressed before Carson returned. How could she be so cool about sleeping with a man she'd just met?

Alana had never slept with a man on the first date, much less married one.

She pressed her fingers to her temples, trying hard to remember anything from the night before.

Nothing.

She shrugged. "Guess we're going to have to take that trip down Memory Lane to figure out more about why someone is threatening us."

"That's right," Chase said from the bedroom door. "Are you ready to go?"

She turned, and her heart flipped.

Chase stood there in dark trousers and a

powder-blue polo shirt that matched the pale blue of his eyes.

Oh, yes, she was beginning to see why she'd taken a step on the wild side. The man inspired wild thoughts with those wickedly beautiful eyes and an even more panty-melting smile.

One look at the handsome, virile man, made Alana suspect she was in more trouble than she'd originally imagined.

But when he held out his hand, she took it.

Chase took Alana's hand and led her to the elevator. "We need to start with what we do remember."

Alana didn't pull her hand free of his as they waited for the elevator doors to open. "While you were in the shower, I thought and thought, but I can't remember anything about you from last night, or any of the events following our meeting."

"Then we need to back up the timeline even more," Chase said.

A bell sounded.

Chase stepped in front of Alana before the elevator doors slid open. The hotel's appearance disguised the fact that all was not well in Cabo San Lucas. The paint was fresh and the decorations bright and cheerful. Those things didn't spell danger to him. The text message on Gina's phone had.

The elevator was empty. Still, he made Alana wait in the hallway while he checked the interior for any signs of tampering. When he was satisfied it was okay, he allowed Alana to enter the elevator car.

She shook her head. "You're taking this protection thing seriously, aren't you?"

"Yes," he said. "So, please, set aside your independence for the sake of survival, and let me go first into places."

"But that would put *you* at risk."

"Better me than you," Chase said. "Apparently, our Text Dude wants a piece of me. He's not above using an innocent woman to get what he wants."

She liked that he wanted to protect her. Alana couldn't imagine Vance stepping in front of a bullet to save her. He probably would have run the other direction and left her behind. "Back to last night…" Alana changed the subject. "What do you last remember?"

"I was with my friend Trevor."

"Who hasn't made an appearance for me to

believe you have a friend named Trevor?" Alana pointed out.

Chase frowned. "You know, you're right." He pulled out his cellphone and texted his buddy.

Chase: Where are you?

Chase slipped his phone into his pocket and continued. "While I wait for his response, we can continue. As I was saying, I arrived in Cabo on a plane with my friend Trevor yesterday around noon. We went to our separate rooms and agreed to meet for drinks and dinner later that afternoon."

"Sounds about like what I remember doing," Alana said. "However, I arrived late yesterday afternoon with Gina."

"Arriving with your friend, instead of the husband you expected to accompany you on your honeymoon," he said, raising one dark eyebrow.

Alana nodded. "I consider it a bullet dodged."

"And I'm a bullet that hit its mark?"

"Something like that." The corners of her lips twitched, a good indication the woman had a sense of humor. Chase liked that in a person. He'd spent so much of his time with his

SEAL team, and, though they participated in serious life-or-death missions, they still managed to laugh and play pranks on each other.

"Continue," she encouraged.

"Trevor and I had enough time to catch some Zs before we went to dinner, which was just as well, because we'd been up the night before in Coronado at McP's Irish Pub. Our old SEAL team threw us a going-away party. Trevor, of course, left several months ago, but I had just processed out."

Alana looked up at him, her eyebrows hiked. "Out of the Navy? You're not on vacation?"

He nodded. "Out completely. If I were a cat, I used up eight lives on Special Operations missions. I wanted to have a life before I reached my expiration date."

"And what do you consider life? Marriage, children, a house with a white picket fence?" Alana asked while staring down at her feet.

"I don't know exactly. I hope I'll know it when I see it. For the most part, I wanted a life where I wasn't being shot at, where I could ride horses and smell the pine sap. I kept in touch with Trevor after he left the military. He went to work in Montana for another SEAL buddy of ours from way back. He's been pulling body-guard assignments. For the most part, they sounded a lot less stressful or dangerous than the missions we'd spent the better part of almost half our lives conducting. Do you know I've never learned to fish? That was one of my goals in coming to Los Cabos. I want to go deep-sea fishing while I'm here."

"You've never fished? Seriously?" Alana shook her head. "Even I've learned to fish, but that's not unusual when you grow up on Maui."

"Maui?" Chase tilted his head and studied her. "Now, that's the life. Growing up on Maui had to be amazing."

Alana nodded. "It was. My father took me fishing on weekends and during the summer until I grew up and moved out of my parents' house. Lately, I've been scuba diving with a friend who happens to be an underwater photographer. She catches fish in pictures instead of on a hook." Alana smiled, her gaze on the stainless-steel walls of the elevator's interior.

Chase shook his head. "My father owned his own machine shop. He rarely took off. And when he did, my mother had a list of chores and things to fix. There never seemed to be time to go fishing or camping like other families did. I guess I wanted that. I thought I might get more of the outdoors when I joined the Navy." He laughed. "I did get a lot more of the outdoors in the sandbox and in jungles. Still, it wasn't the lazy fishing and fun camping I missed as a kid."

Alana shook her head. "I can only imagine. It had to be harder, more intense."

Chase's chest tightened. "When one of my friends was killed on a mission, it hit too close to home. It could've been me. I could've died, never having learned to fish." He grinned as the elevator door opened. "I've scheduled a deep-sea fishing trip with Trevor three days from now."

"You'll love it. Unlike fishing from the shore with my father, where many times we came up empty, most deep-sea fishing trips guarantee you'll catch something." She laughed. "My father rented a boat and took me and my brother fishing off the Maui coast one summer. I caught a small octopus, and my brother caught a six-foot nurse shark." Her smile continued, even after she stopped talking. The smile softened her features.

Chase liked it when she smiled. It made his own heart feel lighter, which made him want to make her smile more often. "Well, that's why I stepped away from the military. I wanted to do those things."

Alana's brows wrinkled. "So, you came to Los Cabos to fish?"

"I came to Cabo to learn how to relax and have a real vacation." The elevator stopped on the ground level, and Chase stepped out first, checking the lobby for any signs of someone who might hurt Alana. "Come on. Let's go out the back door." Again, he took her hand and ushered her out the back door of the lobby. It led to a tiki-style bar and grill on the back patio. "Trevor and I had dinner and came back to the hotel to have a drink." He laid his hands on the bar. "At this bar."

Alana's eyes lit up. "That's what we did. Gina and I ditched our bags as soon as we arrived and came down here. I skipped eating and went straight for the hard stuff." She grimaced. "I can't believe I downed so many shots with nothing else in my stomach."

"You're lucky you didn't end up with alcohol poisoning."

She nodded. "I never drink that much. The

most I drink back on Maui is an occasional glass of wine, a beer or a mild mixed drink."

"So, you had too much. Do you remember anything after that?" Chase asked.

She closed her eyes and thought. "They were playing some music."

The bartender stepped in front of them. "What would you like to drink?" he asked.

"No tequila," Alana said too fast and laughed. "How about a margarita?"

Chase ordered two margaritas.

When the bartender set their drinks in front of them, Chase handed her one and lifted his to his lips for a quick sip. Then he hit up the bartender with the question on both their minds, "Did you work here last night?"

The bartender nodded. "Yes, sir."

Alana quickly swallowed the sip she had just taken. "Oh, good." She leaned across the counter. "What do you remember about us?"

The man frowned. "You were wearing a red dress." His frown cleared, and he pointed at Chase. "You were giving the *señora* lessons on how to salsa."

Alana's gaze whipped to Chase. "Him? He was teaching *me* how to dance to salsa music?

Do you even know how to salsa dance?" She took another sip of her drink.

Chase shrugged. "My dad didn't have time to teach his sons to fish, but my mother took the time to make sure her boys could dance. And she loved the rhythm of the salsa more than the foxtrot or polka."

The bartender laid the check on the counter.

Chase downed half of his drink and then laid his credit card on the counter.

When the bartender gave him a receipt, Chase shoved it into the pocket of his trousers. That's when he felt the crinkle of more paper in his right pocket. He pulled out the wadded slip and read the date on the paper. It had been printed the day before, but the name at the top of the receipt was barely legible.

"Can you read this?" He handed the receipt to Alana.

"I don't know." Alana's eyes narrowed as she studied the print. "It could say 'Cabo Wabo'…"

"That's the bar on the beach," the bartender said. "*Mi hermano*, my brother, is the bartender there. I sent you there after you won the salsa contest here."

"Salsa contest?" Alana's brow wrinkled. "I don't know how to salsa that well."

The bartender's eyes widened. "You danced like a true *Mexicana*." The man raised one hand, cupped his ample belly with the other and moved his feet in the traditional moves of the salsa dance. "*Fuiste magnífico!*"

"But I hardly know how to dance the salsa," Alana insisted.

Chase's lips twitched. "But I do." He took her hand, pulled her against him and showed her.

At first, her body was stiff against his, but soon, she moved to the rhythm of Chase's feet, following him perfectly. What his mind couldn't remember, his body did. "We've danced together," he murmured. He spun her out and back into his arms.

Her eyes widened. "We have! How could I forget this? I've always wanted to learn to dance like this. How did you know?"

"My mother is of Irish descent and always regretted that my father was never around to learn how to dance with her. The woman was on a mission to make sure her boys didn't disappoint the ladies." He danced a few more steps with her and brought her to a stop in his arms. He liked that she didn't pull free immediately. Alana was a perfect fit for his height. She wasn't too short or too tall, and her curves met his planes just right.

She raised her drink and touched it to the edge of his glass. "Kudos to your mother. She knew what a woman wants. So many men don't even bother to learn how to dance." Her cheeks flushed, and she stepped away from him. "But that's not enough to make me want to marry a stranger. Although it puts you right up there in my books."

"Didn't your fiancé take you dancing?" Chase asked.

"Never. He didn't have a rhythmic bone in his body." She snorted. "He even refused to take a lesson to be ready for the first dance at our wedding."

"Not the man for you," Chase said. "You're a natural dancer. Did you take lessons?"

She nodded. "My mother had me in dance class by the time I turned four."

"I could tell." He cupped her cheek. "I've danced with a lot of women, but none were as fluid as you."

The color in her cheeks deepened as she stared up into his eyes. "Thank your mother for me. I've never danced with anyone who could lead. I'm usually the one leading, and I'm not that good."

After they finished their drinks, Chase took her arm and led her toward the garden and the rear exit of the resort. "Maybe, after our annulment, you and I can go dancing."

Alana nodded. "I'd like that. We'll be here a week."

Chase's heart warmed at her positive response. He wanted to spend more time with his wife. "Same here. Trevor's woman is supposed to join us today. Once she arrives, I doubt I'll see him for the rest of my stay."

"Knowing Gina, she'll be occupied with Carson for the duration of our visit."

Chase emerged from the back garden onto a sidewalk that led to the street. He pulled out his cellphone and looked up the bar on the receipt. "It appears to be three miles from here. We can walk or catch a—"

Before he finished his sentence, a taxi pulled to a halt in front of him.

Chase cocked his eyebrows and waved toward the cab. "After you."

Alana slid into the cab and scooted over. "Cabo Wabo, *por favor*."

As Chase bent to slide into the taxi, a shadow shifted at the far corner of the building. He closed the car door and turned to look back. Before he could check out the source of the shadow, the driver shot out into traffic. He swerved around another vehicle, slinging Chase sideways into Alana.

He nearly crushed Alana against the opposite door before he righted himself. "Sorry."

"It's okay," she said, her head ducked as she searched for a seatbelt. "I think our driver has a death *wisshh*—"

The cab swerved back into the opposite lane, flinging Alana across Chase's lap.

Chase gripped her hips and held on as the driver weaved in and out of the traffic in jerky motions.

The cab quickly screeched to a halt in front of the Cabo Wabo. Chase leaped from the cab and pulled Alana out and into his arms.

She clung to him until she got her footing and then stepped away.

Chase had to admit he'd liked having her splayed across his lap for the majority of the five-minute ride. He leaned into the cab and paid the cab driver, who hit the accelerator, almost taking Chase's arm with him.

Chase jumped back, shaking his head.

Alana chuckled. "Who needs a roller coaster when you have cab drivers like that?"

"I hope all the drivers aren't that aggressive," Chase said.

"I don't know." Alana tilted her head as she studied the disappearing taxi. "It certainly added to the Cabo adventure."

Chase laughed. "As if dancing with a stranger, waking up with him in your bed and finding out you're married to him isn't enough adventure?"

"That ride ranked right up there with the rest. I wasn't sure we'd arrive at our destination—alive."

"You have a point." Chase grinned. "Let's walk back. Three miles is just a stretch of the legs."

"Agreed."

Chase took her hand and started to turn toward Cabo Wabo. After having her in his lap for the duration of the cab ride, holding her hand seemed natural. Her palm was warm and dry, and her fingers laced with his, delicate yet strong. He liked the way she felt at his side. He might even miss the woman once their wedding was annulled.

They had yet to take a step when a dark sedan raced toward them.

Chase yanked Alana's hand and dragged her away from the street, shielding her body with his.

The vehicle jumped the curb, running over the sidewalk where they'd just been standing. Chase kept moving, his arm around Alana, hurrying her away from the street and the reckless driver.

The driver jerked the vehicle back onto the street and sped off.

Chase didn't stop running until they were through the entrance of Cabo Wabo, his pulse pounding and short a few years of his life. That had been too near a miss. He'd almost lost his wife before having a chance to get to know her.

CHAPTER 5

"HOLY CRAP," Alana gasped, her heart pounding hard against her ribs. "That was close."

"Too close," Chase said, his mouth set in a grim line, his gaze cast over his shoulder at the disappearing car.

Alana's eyes widened. "You think he was aiming for us?"

"I don't know. But it would pay to be more aware."

One of his hands rested at the small of her back, the other held her hand in his.

Alana was all too aware of the strong hand gripping hers. The man could easily crush her fingers in his, but he didn't. She should have let go and stepped away, but she couldn't. She liked the way his grip felt…firm, like he could handle anything thrown his way. Like moving her out of harm's way in a split second.

As soon as they entered the bar, a voice called out, "Flannigan!"

After being in the glaring sun and nearly run over, Alana had to blink several times before her vision adjusted to the dim lighting of the interior. An ample-breasted, older Hispanic woman hobbled toward Chase with a decided limp, her arms opened wide.

Chase didn't have time to dodge her or move out of the way. Suddenly, he was engulfed in what appeared to be a bone-crushing hug.

"*Mi amigo*," the woman cried. She spoke in rapid-fire Spanish, none of which Alana understood.

A younger woman followed. She appeared to be in her late teens or early twenties. "*Mi madre* said she is very happy you returned today. She is very thankful you helped her yesterday when she fell outside on the street. No one else offered to help. *Muchas gracias, Señor* Flannigan."

The older woman spoke again, winked at Chase and nodded with a smile toward Alana.

Alana frowned, wishing she'd taken the time to learn more Spanish.

"*Mi madre* says you are a gentleman, and your lovely bride is very lucky to have such a handsome husband."

Chase slipped his left arm around Alana and held out his right hand to the young woman. "What's your name?"

"Teresa," she responded.

"Thank you, Teresa. You speak English fluently. Thank you." Chase gave the younger woman a smile that melted Alana's knees and made her wish he'd directed it at her.

Based on how pink Teresa's cheeks turned, she was equally affected.

"And your mother's name?" Chase asked.

"Delores Hernandez," the daughter said.

Chase took the older woman's hand and squeezed it gently. "*Señora* Hernandez, you have a beautiful daughter, and you are very welcome. *De nada.*"

Her daughter's blush deepened, and she stammered a little as she translated, making the older woman's smile stretch across her face.

Señora Hernandez motioned for them to continue into the establishment.

"She welcomes you back to the Cabo

Wabo," Teresa said, "and offers to provide your food and drinks. *Usted no tiene que pagar.*"

"Tell her thank you," Chase said. "But we came to ask questions. You see, we don't remember much about what happened last night while we were here. We had hoped someone could remind us, and maybe we'll remember."

Teresa waved toward the bar at the center of the room. "Juan was here last night after my mother left. He will be able to answer your questions."

Alana marveled at how easily the Navy SEAL charmed the two ladies, both older and younger. When he turned those incredibly blue eyes and his killer smile on someone, she could see how someone could fall in love with him in seconds.

Was that what had happened? Had he smiled at her and turned her knees to mush? Even though he was using his charm on the other women, it affected her as well.

The thought made her frown. She wasn't supposed to be falling for the guy. She was supposed to be discovering how they'd ended up married, why someone was threatening them and how they could end their short-lived marriage. Alana squared her shoulders and crossed to the bartender.

"*Buenos días,* Juan," Alana said with a smile. "Do you remember us from last night?"

The bartender grinned. "*Sí, si.*" He nodded toward her. "Alana and Chase." He spread his arms wide. "*Mis amigos,* what can I get you?"

"We're having a hard time remembering what happened last night," Alana said.

Juan nodded and winked. "Ah, the tequila. You two had several shots while here."

"We did?" Alana cringed. No wonder her head still hurt.

"*Sí,* and then the *señor* started the conga line."

Alana shot a glance at Chase and laughed. "You salsa dance and you conga?"

He shrugged. "I've been known…"

"And you help women in distress." Alana shook her head. "Is there anything you can't do?"

"I can't convince you I'm an okay kinda guy." He winked and turned to the bartender. "Was there any trouble here last night? Did I get into a fight?"

Juan frowned. "You, *señor*? No. You and the *señora* had everyone laughing and having a good time. You closed the bar down at two o'clock in the morning."

"Closed?" Alana asked.

"*Sí, señora.*"

She didn't try to correct Juan regarding the *señora* reference, although she wanted to. Correcting him would only delay getting to the bottom of what had happened the night before.

"You did not want the party to stop." Juan smiled. "Everyone moved to La Casa Loca, where they stay open until four o'clock in the morning."

Alana exchanged a silent glance with Chase. Perhaps, they were finally getting somewhere in their investigation.

Chase's lips tightened briefly. "Where is La Casa Loca?"

"Not far down the beach from here." Juan laughed. "You led the conga line all the way there, stopping halfway for a short time." He grinned. "I watched from the outside patio."

"*Gracias, amigo.*" Chase held out his hand to Juan.

"*De nada*, my friend." Juan shook his hand. "Come back later, *sí?* You are good for business."

Chase smiled. "We'll be back, but maybe not tonight."

Juan nodded and touched his temple. "The tequila is strong, *sí?*"

"*Sí,*" Chase said. He hooked Alana's arm and guided her out the door leading to the beach.

"Sounds like we had the time of our lives." Alana began to regret that she couldn't remember anything about their night together.

"I'm thinking it was a damned shame I forgot most of it."

"Most?" Alana frowned. "Do you remember any of it?"

He squinted at the sunshine glaring off the water. "I swear I can hear the music from the conga line. And I recognized Mama Delores, though I couldn't remember her name."

Alana sighed. "That's more than I got."

They walked along the path leading to the beach in silence.

When they reached the sand, Alana automatically kicked off her flip-flops and bent to pick them up.

Chase did the same. Then he captured her hand in his, as if he had every right to do so.

Instinctively, Alana knew that if she didn't want him to hold her hand, he would release it at once. She hated to admit it, but she liked that he held her hand. Well, *hated* was a strong word. She didn't *like* that she was softening toward the man who'd obviously tricked her into marrying him. How else had she ended up wearing a wedding ring with a marriage license to prove it had happened? No woman in her right mind would marry a guy she'd only just met.

That was the problem. She hadn't been in her right mind. Her brain had been soaked in tequila. She was surprised she hadn't succumbed to alcohol poisoning.

"You say you just got off active duty?" Alana asked, curious about the man she'd married.

"Yes, ma'am." He looked out to the sea. "I served for eleven years as a Navy SEAL."

She frowned. "Why didn't you go until retirement at twenty years?"

He didn't answer for a while. Alana thought he was ignoring her question until he answered, "I used to love the adrenaline rush of going into battle. I lived for the fight, for the challenge."

"What changed?" she asked softly.

His hand tightened on hers. "I lost too many of my friends. Some of them had taken the plunge and dared to marry and have children. They were my brothers. And they had family who loved them. Those wives lost their husbands. Those children will never know their fathers."

Alana's heart squeezed hard in her chest at the sadness in Chase's voice. "Is that why you didn't marry?" she asked quietly.

He nodded. "I figured it wasn't fair to any woman to put her through that kind of loss."

"What if the woman knows what she's signing up for and loves her man enough to go into it with her eyes wide open? Don't you think it should be her choice?"

"No woman could understand the danger we faced on every deployment. And we were gone more than we were at home. She'd have been on her own more often than not."

"Again, why wouldn't you give her the choice?" Alana lifted her shoulders and let them fall. "Not all women are weak and dependent on a man to survive. We're not all wimps."

"Lots of my friends' marriages ended in divorce," Chase said. "Their spouses couldn't handle the loneliness. They found other men to make them happy."

Alana's lips pressed together. "They weren't the right women for your friends."

"Yeah, well, I didn't meet a woman who fit that bill." Chase nodded toward a building ahead with a huge, garish red-and-orange sign proclaiming it La Casa Loca.

Rather than continue to the bar, he turned her toward a small shop several structures short of their destination.

"Where are we going?" Alana asked, trotting to keep up.

"I don't feel good about wandering around out in the open, especially after the near miss with the car in front of the Cabo Wabo bar."

Alana shivered. "Me either."

Chase nodded. "And if Text Dude is looking for us, I don't want to make it any easier for him to find us before our rendezvous time."

Alana glanced over her shoulder. "Do you really think someone could be following us?"

His jaw hardened. "It's possible. They knew we were at the hotel. The bad driver could've followed our cab. No matter what, it wouldn't hurt to have a disguise." He stepped through the door into a cornucopia of souvenirs and junk from Cabo San Lucas, from magnets and key chains to beach towels and floppy hats.

He selected two brightly colored baseball caps with Cabo San Lucas embroidered across the front and two pairs of large, round sunglasses. He paid for them with his credit card and then handed her one of each. "Think you can hide your blond hair in that hat?"

Alana bent over, twisted her hair into a tight knot and jammed the baseball cap over her head, tucking any loose strands inside. When she straightened, she grinned. "It won't cover all of it, but at least, from a distance, it won't be as noticeable." Alana put on the sunglasses.

Chase settled his cap on his head and wore the glasses. Even in the touristy getup, he was still sexy as hell.

He touched a finger to the bill of her cap. "Anyone ever mention that you look like a cute tomboy with your hair pulled up like that?"

She tilted her head. "Is that a good thing or a bad thing?"

"All good, sweetheart. Maybe, too good. I'm thinking I like this outfit almost as much as the red dress."

Her cheeks heated and warmth spread throughout her body.

"But as cute as you are, you might want to stay here while I go check out La Casa Loca."

She shook her head. "Nope. I'm going with you. If this is the place where the pot got stirred, you're not going in there alone."

He frowned. "And if it gets dangerous? What then?"

"I'll be your back up. I'll call the police." When he arched his brow, she raised her hands. "I don't know. I can hit someone with a chair or a bottle of booze. All I know is you're not going in there alone."

He chuckled. "You're cute when you go all badass." Chase bent and kissed the tip of her nose.

Alana stood still, her lips parting slightly.

Then Chase kissed her mouth, taking advantage of her parted lips to sweep his tongue past her teeth to slide the length of hers.

Too shocked to think, and too mesmerized to push away, Alana dug her fingers into his blue polo shirt and drew him closer, deepening the kiss. Her mouth moved with his as though following a muscle memory. She didn't even realize she'd kissed him back until Chase lifted his head.

"Finally, something I remember clearly," he whispered.

Sweet heaven, so did she.

He turned her toward the beach, took her hand in his and walked out to the sand.

Two doors down from the souvenir shop, they came to a tiny little hut with the words "Wedding Chapel Open 24 Hours" written in broad, baby-blue letters.

Alana and Chase halted at the same time.

She pointed to the chapel. "You don't think…"

"It's way too much of a coincidence," Chase said. "Would they have some kind of register?"

"There's only one way to know for sure." Alana drew in a deep breath.

Chase's hand tightened around hers, and they walked into the chapel.

CHAPTER 6

Chase recognized the place as soon as they entered, even before his eyes adjusted to the dim lighting inside. He'd been there before.

"Welcome to the Wedding Chapel." The proprietor's gaze zeroed in on the rings they wore. "You look like a happy couple. Are you looking to renew your vows? We offer a discount package for vow renewals."

"No, thank you," Alana said.

"*Buenos días, Señor.*" Chase held out his hand. "Were you working here last night?"

"No, *señor,* that would be *mi hermano, Julio.*"

Alana smiled at the man. "Do you have a registry that lists the couples who've been married in this chapel?"

"*Sí, señora.* We do." He led them to a large

white book on a table near the rear of the chapel.

Chase knew what they'd find. He remembered being there. He remembered standing at the altar, facing Alana in her red dress and a borrowed white veil. That memory came back to him with all the force of a freight train. He'd bought rings, married her, kissed her and signed the papers all in the matter of a few minutes.

Alana bent over the book and dragged her finger down the page to the bottom. For a long moment, she stared at the two signatures on the line. "We really did it."

"Yes, we did." He didn't tell her he remembered. Nor did he tell her how he'd felt at the moment he'd said I do, because he felt it all over again. That feeling of rightness. That this was a woman he could trust with his heart, and who would never leave him for another man because she was lonely and insecure. She was the one.

All those thoughts raced through his head as he stared down at his signature on the page.

And Alana wanted to have their union annulled.

That knowledge made a hole in his chest where his heart should have been.

"What were we thinking?" Alana stared at their signatures, shaking her head.

"Blame it on the tequila," Chase murmured. He took her hand and led her toward the exit. On the wall beside the door leading out to the beach were photos of some of the couples who'd been married in the little chapel. Dead center was an instant photo of Alana and Chase, just like the one they'd found in his hotel room. Alana wore the red dress and a funny little white veil. He wore black trousers and the white polo shirt he'd worn on the flight from California to Cabo. They'd smiled for the camera, appearing like all the other couples posted on the wall—happy.

Why had they woken up completely devoid of these memories? Well, at least he could remember the wedding ceremony and kissing the bride. With her hand in his, he wanted to pull her into his arms and test that kiss again. If he did, would he recapture the feeling of right-ness? Would she feel the same? And would it trigger her memory?

Alana paused to study the photos. Chase knew the exact moment she spotted theirs. She stiffened, and a small gasp escaped her lips. "Just like the one in your room," she whispered. "It wasn't a prank." By now, the reality of their marriage was etched in stone. The rings, the marriage certificate, signatures in the chapel registry and the photos would have been too much of a coincidence.

"Julio said that a couple came in last night with a mile-long conga line." The proprietor chuckled. "He prides himself on judging whether or not a couple's marriage will stand the test of time. Those two were completely head-over-heels for each other. They'll be together until death do they part."

Alana's fingers tightened around Chase's hand, but she didn't pull free. "We should be going. Thank you for letting us in."

"My pleasure. And remember, if you want to renew your vows, it's half the cost of a wedding package."

Alana's cheeks reddened, and she ducked her head.

The proprietor opened his arms wide. "We are here to help give a jumpstart to every couple's dreams of marriage and happiness by taking the work out of wedding planning."

Alana slipped through the door and out

onto the sand, still holding onto Chase's hand. "We're almost to La Casa Loca," she said unnecessarily.

Chase could clearly see the structure.

"Do you think it's safe to enter?" she asked, her expression impossible to read behind the big, round sunglasses.

He studied the building ahead. Tourists sat on the outdoor patio, drinking, eating and smiling happily. On the beach around the establishment, young people lounged in everything from Speedos to bikinis and one-piece swimsuits. Mothers chased children into the waves, and families gathered around beach umbrellas to share sandwiches or to apply sunscreen. "I think it'll be fairly safe during the light of day. But I would prefer you to stay outside in case my guy is inside, determined to take me down."

Even before he finished his statement, Alana was shaking her head. "We've been over this before. I'm just as much a target as you are, and you need someone watching your back. Besides, they won't recognize us in these ridiculous disguises. The guy who married us sure didn't connect us to the couple in the photograph." She gave him a fake smile. "See?

We're just a couple of tourists, going into an establishment for a drink."

Chase brushed a finger across her cheek. "You know, you're pretty special." Then he bent and touched his lips to hers in a feather-soft kiss. "I'm beginning to see why I married you so quickly."

Alana raised her hand to her lips. "Why did you do that?"

He grinned. "Do what? Do this?" Chase dropped another kiss on her lips. But it wasn't enough. Before he could think through his actions, he pulled her into his arms and deepened the kiss. Oh, yeah. His lips couldn't forget the sensation of her mouth against his.

Alana stood still, her hands resting against Chase's chest. When he started to pull away, she curled her fingers into his polo shirt and dragged him closer.

Chase obliged, happy to kiss this woman and hoping she would remember at least part of the night before.

He swept his tongue across the seam of her lips.

Alana opened her mouth on a sigh, giving Chase the opportunity to dart in and caress her tongue in a long, sensuous kiss.

For a long moment, they stood in the sand, frozen in time, kissing like long-lost lovers.

When at last Chase raised his head to take a breath, he leaned his forehead against hers. "I remember this."

Alana stared at his chest, the sunglasses shielding her eyes. Finally, she shook her head. "I don't remember any of this." Then she stepped backward, out of Chase's embrace. "We need to move on if we're going to discover what happened before your midnight rendezvous." She set out across the sand at a brisk pace.

Chase hurried to catch up. When he reached for her hand, she brushed his aside and kept walking. *What the hell?* He could not have been mistaken by her earlier response. Alana had returned the kiss with as much fervor as he'd given. What had he done wrong to deserve the cold shoulder now?

ALANA CHARGED AHEAD, determined to get to the bar, learn what they could and get the hell out of the mess they'd landed in. She couldn't believe she'd married a stranger within hours of meeting him. Not only would her father go ballistic, but he'd also likely hire a hit man to take out the man who'd dared marry his daughter so quickly. He'd be convinced the man was after one thing only—Daddy's money.

She'd have to remind her father that money alone didn't ensure a marriage. Vance was proof of that. When it had come to the actual wedding ceremony, he'd skipped out with someone else rather than marry her.

Alana frowned. Or had her father paid him off? Had he paid Vance to skip out on her wedding and go off with the wedding planner? The moment the thought came to her, it left. No. Her father had approved of Vance. He'd pushed for the marriage as much as she had.

Her father would disapprove of Chase immediately upon meeting him. The fact he hadn't had a hand in selecting him for his daughter would play a huge part in that disapproval. Dwayne Neal, a multimillionaire, liked to control every aspect of his daughter's life. Perhaps that was why Alana liked Gina so much. Her father hadn't chosen Gina to be her friend. They'd been friends since they'd met at a party in Honolulu. Gina had come as a guest of a guest. It galled her father that he didn't know Gina and couldn't find enough dirt on her to keep her out of Alana's life.

Thank God, Gina had been there when her wedding day fell apart. Gina and her other friend, Kimo, had helped Alana out of her dress and into the red one, grabbed her suitcase and bundled her and Gina into a taxi before her father had arrived to berate her for letting Vance slip away. He would have found a way to make it her fault that her fiancé had eloped with the wedding planner. He never understood when people didn't do what he expected of them.

Alana didn't go to great lengths to displease her father, but she found a bit of backbone and a rebellious streak running through her veins when her father cinched the reins too tightly. Perhaps that was one of the reasons she'd gravitated toward the handsome SEAL.

Her father wouldn't have liked her hanging out with a man trained in combat. A man he hadn't met and couldn't control. Yeah, Daddy would be livid when he discovered she'd married someone other than Vanishing Vance.

As they neared La Casa Loca, Chase hooked his arm through Alana's and slowed her down.

"We're not in a race," he reminded her. "We're tourists coming in for a drink at the bar."

Alana slowed her steps. "Right. Tourists. With a murderer wanting to off us for some reason we can't remember." She threw him a sideways grin, albeit a forced grin. "Got it."

She liked the feel of his arm hooked in hers. Liked the hardness of his muscles against her body, and she wondered, not for the first time—and probably not the last—what it felt like to make love with him. Try as she might, she couldn't remember.

But she had remembered his kiss. Her core coiled and heated. No woman could forget a kiss like that. That kiss fired up memories of a dance that had ended in a similar kiss. She remembered the fire in her veins as he'd spun her around the floor, the way his hips had moved to the rhythm of the music, and how he'd dipped her low to the ground, crushing his lips to hers in a searing kiss that had left her panties damp and her heart pounding to the beat of the Latin music.

Even as she walked into the bar, her heart thrummed to that tune in her head, firing up her nerves and making her pulse beat hard against her eardrums.

Once inside, Alana reached for her sunglasses. The dimness of the interior made it hard to distinguish between the shapes of people or furniture.

"Might want to keep those on." Chase covered her hands with his and guided the glasses back onto her nose. "Your eyes are unforgettable."

"You managed to forget them," she reminded him.

"Yeah, but I was drunk. We can't expect La Casa Loca staff to have been in the same inebriated state last night. We're better off if they don't know who we are."

"If we don't want them to know who we are, how will we ask about last night?" Alana asked.

"Leave it to me," Chase said. He made a beeline for the bar and settled her onto a stool before sliding onto one himself.

The bartender took their orders and delivered a Salty Dog for Chase and a beer for Alana.

"I would've guessed you as a whiskey drinker," Alana said.

"And I would've guessed more margaritas for you."

"Normally, I would have a margarita." She lifted a shoulder. "But after all the tequila I had last night…" She pinched the bridge of her nose. "My head still hurts."

"And normally, I would drink a whiskey. But now that I'm out of the military, I have to watch what I drink. I figure grapefruit juice is healthy, right?" Chase lifted his drink and grinned. "And, like you, my head is numb from the tequila last night."

Alana laughed. "The grapefruit juice might be better for you, but the vodka…not so much."

The bartender drifted off to wait on another customer. He returned a few minutes later. "Anything else?" he asked while wiping the counter with a cloth.

Chase smiled at the short, meaty Hispanic man. "We heard there was some excitement here last night."

With a shrug, the bartender continued wiping.

Alana gritted her teeth and waited for Chase to continue.

"Were you here?" Chase asked.

Again, the bartender shrugged.

After a quick glance around the bar, Chase leaned forward. "Was there a fight?"

The man nodded, glanced around the interior of the bar, just like Chase had a moment before, and leaned closer. "We had a visit from the Jalisco cartel. Raul Delgado, one of the leaders of the cartel, got into a fight with a tourist. The tourist beat the shit out of Delgado. Delgado wouldn't back down. He was very angry that he got bested in front of his men."

"Why didn't his men stick up for him?" Alana asked.

"They did," the bartender said. "Only the tourist they targeted was a better fighter than Delgado and his men."

"Good to know," Chase said. "Does this cartel hang out here often?"

"Delgado likes to flirt with the pretty tourists," the bartender said.

Alana tilted her head. "The Cabo police don't keep them out? I thought they were pretty good at protecting the tourism trade."

The bartender snorted. "The last policeman who dared stand up to Delgado ended up hanging from a bridge."

Alana swallowed hard. With all the nice trappings of the tourist hotels and resorts, there was a seedier side to Cabo San Lucas.

And it appeared that seedier side was infiltrating the tourist haunts. "Do you know how many people are a part of the Jalisco cartel?"

"One, maybe two hundred," the bartender said. "And that's just in the Cabo area."

Her belly knotted as Alana fought to stay upright. "Do they ever show up in the same place all at once?" she asked, her voice squeaking slightly.

The bartender's eyes narrowed. "Why so much interest in the cartel? The cartels are part of life in Mexico. We learn to stay clear or give them the payola they demand to leave us alone."

"Is that what you do? Pay the Jalisco cartel to leave you alone?" Chase asked.

A frown settled on the man's thick brow. "You ask too many questions. If you don't want another drink, you go. We don't want trouble here."

Chase slid an American one-hundred-dollar bill across the counter. "Thank you for your time." He got up, helped Alana off her bar stool and walked out of the bar.

"I remember what happened last night," Chase said, his jaw tightening.

"Why is it you can remember, but I can't?"

He touched a hand to his bruised cheek. "I remembered a Hispanic man hitting me. When that memory returned, I remembered why he hit me."

Alana stopped and faced Chase. "Why did he hit you?"

Chase cupped her elbow and steered her around the back of the building.

"Where are we going?"

"I need to know the layout of the building and the surrounding area."

Alana dug her heels into the ground and stopped. "You're not actually considering showing up for Delgado, are you?"

"If I want him off my back and yours, I may have to confront him."

Her pulse quickened, and her chest grew tight. "You heard the bartender. And you've seen news reports. Confrontations with the cartel don't end well."

Chase didn't look at her. He scanned the immediate vicinity, studying it as if committing every nook and cranny to memory. "He won't leave us alone unless I show up here."

"Then we should leave Cabo." She touched his arm. "Now."

"I have a feeling leaving won't be an option.

He probably has contacts at the airport. He had them at the hotel. If I'm not wrong, that near-miss in front of Cabo Wabo was one of his people. He wants a piece of me and won't be satisfied until he gets it."

"So, you're just going to march into a hive of cartel thugs? Alone and unarmed?" Alana shook her head, her heart hammering, her mind spinning with the potential scenarios. "Why did you get into a fight with Delgado?" she asked. "You don't strike me as someone who goes around picking fights with cartel members. Perhaps it's all some big misunderstanding."

A smile twisted into a grimace on Chase's face. "What do most men fight over?"

"Money, cars and women?" Alana lifted her hands, palms facing upward. "You name it."

Chase chuckled. "Point taken. This time it was a woman."

"A woman?" Alana frowned, her fingers curling, her nails ready to dig into any woman who had come close to Chase. "What woman?"

He turned to face her and lifted one of her hands. "You."

The soft tone of his voice and the way he

laced his fingers with hers made her weak-kneed and ready to fall into his arms. "Me?" she said, though the sound came out as more of a squeak than a word.

"You," Chase repeated. "I hit the head, the bathroom, after so much beer and tequila. By the time I came back, Delgado had cornered you at the bar and was hitting on you."

"But I wouldn't have given him the time of day if I'd just married you."

"Apparently, you were trying to give him the brush-off, but he wasn't taking no for an answer. About the time I saw what was happening, he grabbed your arm." He turned her palm up and pressed his lips to the lifeline at the center. "I distinctly recall the rush of blood through my veins and the heat about to explode out of my head."

"You were jealous?" Alana's heart seized in her chest, and she held her breath, afraid to breathe until he answered.

"Raging jealousy. I recall it wasn't a pretty feeling. I marched up to Delgado, clamped a hand to his shoulder and spun him around."

Alana gasped. "I'm surprised he didn't stick a knife into you at that moment."

"I didn't give him time to think. I slammed him up against the bar and told him you were my wife and to leave you the hell alone."

Her heart thrilled at Chase's words and chilled at the same time. "Delgado could've killed you."

"Oh, he took a swing and missed. Then he grabbed a bottle from the bar and hit me here." Chase pointed to the bruise on his cheek. "I knocked the bottle out of his hand. It flew across the room and hit one of his cartel groupies."

"Sweet Jesus." Alana pressed a hand to her lips. "You really weren't thinking."

"Nope. I was in pure, primal reactionary mode." Chase stared down into her eyes, his gaze intense, his jaw set in stone. "Someone was hurting my wife. I wouldn't stand for it. Not on my watch."

"So, is it true? You beat the shit out of Delgado?"

Chase grimaced. "I didn't intend to, but he kept swinging. I blocked and swung back."

"You really are insane," Alana said. "The bartender said Delgado's people tried to help him, which means you fought more than one of them."

"They tried," he shoved a hand through his hair. "But I was in full kick-ass mode."

"Wow. I suppose I should be grateful." Alana shook her head. "But you really set yourself up for retribution. You barely knew me. Why didn't you just let me defend myself?"

"You were trying, but Delgado was dragging you toward the exit."

"Well then, thank you," Alana said. Vague memories tugged at her mind but refused to solidify. "Do you think the bartender will let Delgado know we were asking questions?"

"If he does, I'm not worried about it. We need to know what we're up against. Delgado already knows. Apparently, he didn't have as much to drink as we did last night." He lifted her hand to his lips and pressed a kiss to her knuckles. "I'm sorry I got you into this mess, but I'm going to get you out of it. I promise."

"You didn't get me into this mess. Delgado did that." Alana's insides heated at the touch of Chase's lips on her knuckles. "Sounds to me like Delgado was going to take off with me, whether I liked it or not." She lifted her hand to the bruise on his face. "You saved me."

"And put you into more danger by doing

so." He cupped her cheek in his palm and stared down at her.

His blue eyes were so blue that Alana felt as if she could fall into them and never want to come back out. Yes, she could see how she'd fallen so quickly for this man. He was every woman's dream come true—he was handsome, he could dance, he was kind to old women, and he'd taken on a drug cartel to save his woman. Her breath caught in her throat.

His woman.

How ironic was it that she was trying to get out of the marriage most women would love to be in? Hell, she couldn't hold him to the vows, knowing they'd been spoken while shit-faced drunk. He'd said it himself that he wouldn't have married her had he been sober.

After all she'd learned about Chase, the thought of annulling their marriage didn't hold the same appeal as it had a few hours earlier. To be fair, she had to. No man should marry when he was drunk. She'd been stone-cold sober when she'd considered marrying Vance, and that decision had been stupider than marrying a complete stranger after several rounds of tequila shots.

No matter. The marriage would be

annulled before they left Cabo San Lucas. *If* they left in one piece. First, they had to get past the midnight deadline with Delgado, a badass affiliated with one of the most violent cartels in Mexico.

CHAPTER 7

CHASE USHERED Alana along the beach to the next big resort, rather than walking along the street where they could be targeted in a drive-by shooting. Once at the resort, they asked the concierge to call a cab.

Within minutes, the cab arrived. Chase bundled Alana inside, and they were whisked away, heading back to their resort compound several blocks away.

"What's your plan, Mr. Flannigan?" Alana asked as soon as the cab pulled away from the curb.

"I'm not sure yet. I want to convene with Trevor and Carson to see if they have some ideas as to how to handle a confrontation with the cartel."

"Should we go to the American Consulate or something?" she asked. "Do they even have a consulate here in Cabo?"

He rested his back against the seat and scraped a hand over his face. "I don't know. But I can't see that being much help, unless we want to hole up in their building." His eyes narrowed. "Actually, that might be a good idea. While I'm dealing with Delgado, you could be safe in the consulate, if they have one here."

"Nope." Alana crossed her arms over her chest. "I'm not hiding in some government building, while you're taking one for the team, namely for me."

Chase frowned. "He's not after you so much as me, and I can't have you tagging along to this event. It's not a conga line with a bunch of drunks. These cartels mean business. They shoot first and ask questions later, if at all."

"If you're going," she poked a thumb at her chest, "I'm going."

No way was Chase taking her to the confrontation with Delgado. "If you're there, you put me at greater risk. I can't defend myself if I'm worried about you. They might take you hostage and use you to manipulate me."

"Then I'll come in disguise. I'll be a regular tourist in the right place at the wrong time."

Before she finished talking, he was already shaking his head. "You know they're armed with machine guns. They've been known to shoot innocent tourists on the beach with those kinds of weapons."

"I don't care." She lifted her chin. "I'm just as much responsible for this situation as you are." She threw back her shoulders. "I'm going, even if I have to disguise myself as a dog and bark for treats."

Chase pressed his lips into a thin line. He admired the fact that she felt just as compelled to confront Delgado as he did, and she was fearless in her desire to help, but he couldn't have her anywhere near when this shit went down. If he wanted to even the odds a little, he had to come up with a plan to surprise the cartel thug. With only three SEALs, they didn't stand a chance against even a third of the cartel members in the Cabo area. Yeah, they were highly trained combatants, but ten or twenty-to-one odds were impossible. "We'll discuss it later," he said, though he had no intention of backing down and allowing her to accompany them to La Casa Loca that night.

Back at the hotel, Chase hustled Alana into the lobby and to the elevator, keeping her close to him, should Delgado or one of his men be lurking nearby, waiting for Chase and Alana to show up. They made it into the elevator with no problems along the way.

On their floor, Alana stepped out of the elevator beside Chase and looked both ways. "Which room? Mine or yours?"

Chase stepped past her. "Yours. I've texted Trevor. He said he'll be here shortly."

"Hopefully, Gina will know where Carson is," Alana said.

Chase nodded. "I could use all the firepower I can get. We can ask him if he has any weapons. I really don't want to go in empty-handed, if that's the path we choose."

"You might be out of luck on the weapons. I'm sure neither you nor your buddy got through customs carrying pistols, automatic rifles and machine guns. Plus, I have no idea what Carson brought across the border."

"True. But I have the Ka-Bar knife I packed in my checked bag, and I'll bet Trevor didn't leave home without his."

Alana shook her head. "Knives against automatic weapons…? I'm not feeling really good about this. You don't have any high-powered friends in this part of Mexico, do you? Maybe a connection with an opposing cartel or something?"

Chase blew out a long breath. "Afraid not." He wondered if they still had time to call in a favor from his new boss, Hank Patterson. "Let me get on the phone and see if I can get any assistance in this matter."

"We don't have a lot of time." Alana shot a glance at her watch. "It's just past noon. We have less than eleven hours until midnight. We could use a miracle right about now."

As much as he liked the sound of Alana referring to them as *we,* he still had no intention of bringing her with him to La Casa Loca that night.

Chase let Alana slide her key card over the door lock but set her to the side and entered first.

"Hey, it's my room," Alana groused.

Chase paused with his hand on the doorknob. "How often have you breached a room that could be filled with hostiles?"

"Every time I walked into my father's office," she muttered.

"Did he shoot at you?" Chase asked.

"Not with bullets." She rolled her eyes. "Okay. You've proven your point. You can clear the room before I enter."

Chase gave her a curt nod and entered the suite, moving quickly and quietly from room to room until he was certain it was enemy-free.

Alana entered. "I'm going to freshen up and then order something for us to eat through room service."

While Alana was in the bathroom, Chase placed a call to his new boss in Montana.

On the first ring, Hank answered, "Patterson speaking,"

"Hank, Chase Flannigan here," he said.

"Chase. Good to hear from you. But I thought you were on vacation. You shouldn't be calling me until you get back." He paused for a second. "You're not in Montana, are you?"

"No, sir," Chase said. "I'm in Mexico, and I've run into a bit of a challenge I was hoping you might be willing to give me some advice on or help with."

"Shoot," Hank said, his tone as authoritative as any SEAL commander Chase had served under.

He had just finished explaining the situation to Hank when he heard the water shut off in the bathroom. "Any help or advice you can give me is welcome," he ended.

Hank whistled. "Cartels are a bad deal. Let me put a few heads together on this, and I'll get back to you."

"Thank you, sir. Again, any advice would be helpful."

"You'll hear from me in less than an hour," Hank promised and hung up.

"Who was that?" Alana walked out of the bedroom into the sitting area. "I hope it was room service. I'm starving."

"Sorry, it wasn't." He lifted the house phone to call room service. "Pizza or sandwiches all right?"

She nodded. "Either sounds great. But if it's pizza, make it pepperoni. I really like pepperoni, but I rarely get to choose what I like."

He smiled. "A woman after my own heart." Chase ordered a pepperoni pizza with double pepperoni. When he set the phone down, he studied Alana. "Why don't you get to choose what you like on your pizza?"

She drew in a breath and let it out. "My father gets heartburn with pepperoni, and my ex-fiancé wouldn't eat pizza unless it was some fancy kind with sun-dried tomatoes and spinach. All I ever wanted was a fast-food-chain pizza with pepperoni."

"Why didn't you ask for what you wanted?"

"I was always overruled by dominating men. When I was a teen, I'd sneak out of the house and use my father's sports car to pick up my favorite pizza, take it to a park and eat half of it by myself. The other half, I'd hide in my backpack and carry up to my room to eat later."

"As an adult, you couldn't get what you wanted?"

She shrugged. "Not when I was with either of them."

He frowned. "You do like pepperoni, right? You're not just settling on it because I like it, are you?"

She smiled. "Not at all. It's my favorite. And if you recall, I chose pepperoni before you said what you liked. How would I know whether or not it's your favorite?"

"That's right, you did choose pepperoni first. Must be some residual brain lapses from overindulging." He grinned. "And don't worry. Pepperoni is my all-time favorite."

The handle on the door to the suite jiggled.

Chase's attention shot to the door. He held

out a hand to keep Alana from approaching it. "Stay back," he whispered and hurried toward it.

The door burst open, and Gina entered, followed by Carson, Trevor Anderson and Anderson's pregnant wife, Lana.

"Look who I found." Gina dropped her purse on one of the sofas and flopped down beside it. "Seems SEALs are like magnets. They gravitate toward each other. Carson spotted Trevor from across the lobby."

"Hey, Chase." Trevor grinned, guiding his wife to the other end of the sofa. "Gina tells me you've made an enemy."

"Glad to see you made the flight safely, Lana," Chase said. "And yes, I've acquired an enemy. I could use some help, but I'm not sure how involved I want you to be. You have a baby on the way. Now is not a good time for you to waltz into a cartel rumble."

Trevor's eyebrows shot up. "True, but then, I can't let you go in by yourself," Trevor said. "Cartel trouble, huh? Why don't you skip it altogether?"

"Because I can't trust that Raul Delgado will leave Alana alone."

Trevor smiled and crossed the room to

Alana. "Pardon my friend's rudeness." He stuck out his hand. "I'm Trevor Anderson." He shook Alana's hand and turned toward his wife. "And this is my beautiful wife, Lana."

Alana smiled at Lana. "Nice to meet you."

"Did you say Raul Delgado?" Carson stood behind the couch, his hands resting on Gina's shoulders. "As in the Jalisco cartel's leader, Raul Delgado?"

Chase nodded, his lips forming a tight line. "The one and only."

Carson whistled. "I've been here long enough to know you don't piss off anyone in the Jalisco cartel."

"Yeah, well, he was hitting on my wife," Chase said.

"Wife?" Trevor frowned. "What wife?"

"You just met her." Chase's lips twisted in a wry smile. "Apparently, I went on a bender last night, danced the salsa with this woman, closed down one bar and formed a conga line that stretched all the way down the beach to a twenty-four-hour wedding chapel where we tied the knot, and then ended up in La Casa Loca where I crossed Raul Delgado."

Trevor's eyes widened with Chase's explanation. "Holy shit, man. All that in one night?"

He shook his head. "I can't leave you alone for a minute, can I? What are you going to do when I'm not around to bail you out of jail or trouble?"

Chase frowned. "Really, I don't want you to bail me out of this one. I'm afraid it's more than you or I can handle."

"Delgado is one bad mother fucker. He's known for stealing young girls and selling them into the sex trade. I hear he makes millions trafficking drugs and humans across the border into the United States." Carson raised a hand. "That being said, you can count me in, if it helps. I've been bored since I got here. I could use a little action."

"Thanks, but even three of us can't go up against an entire cartel." Chase paced the floor, head down, thinking.

"One of my specialties when I was in the SEALs was explosives. I can make things go boom with practically nothing," Carson offered. "You don't meet him until midnight, do you?"

Chase nodded. "Midnight. But we'd have to sneak in, plant the explosives and hope we didn't hurt anyone else. He's asked to meet behind La Casa Loca. That's a pretty popular tourist spot. We could create a lot of collateral damage if we go around blowing up shit."

"Not to mention, if you kill civilians and tourists," Gina piped in, "the Mexican government would lock you up and throw away the key."

"Or turn you over to the cartel," Carson said. "They don't like dealing with them any more than we do. Half the time, they pay them to leave folks alone."

Chase met Alana's gaze. "Like the bartender said. He pays the cartel to leave him alone. Without weapons, we don't stand a chance. From what I've heard, the cartel has everything from semi-automatic rifles to submachine guns. They aren't afraid to employ them in crowded tourist areas, either."

"Cabo is dependent on tourism, as are lots of other places in Mexico," Carson said. "They've lost a lot of business and millions of tourism dollars due to cartel shootings, kidnappings and hangings."

"You'd think the government would clean up the cartels before they go broke," Lana said.

Carson laughed. "Unfortunately, the men in charge of the government can be as corrupt as the cartels, and if they don't go along with the thugs, they're killed."

"Why did we come here for our delayed honeymoon?" Lana pushed to her feet, her brow furrowed. "Should we catch the next flight home to Montana?"

Trevor lifted her hand to his lips. "If you want to go home, I'll get us on the next plane out."

She frowned. "I didn't fly all the way to Mexico to turn around and fly home the next day. I want to put my swollen feet in the sand and swim in the ocean." She swept a hand across her small baby bump. "But I don't want to put our baby at risk."

"I'm calling now," Trevor pulled his phone out of his pocket.

Lana covered his hand with hers. "No," she said. "I refuse to believe it's as bad as all that. Tonight's the deadline. Let's wait and see what happens."

"If we stay, I'm going to help out my buddy," Trevor said, "once we come up with a plan that doesn't involve getting killed." He shot a glance toward Chase. "You do have a plan, don't you?"

Chase shook his head. "Unless you have a

stash of weapons in your suitcase, I'm fresh out of ideas."

Carson raised a hand. "I might know where someone, who will remain unnamed, might have a stash of illegally acquired weapons."

"Yeah?" Chase looked up, hopefully. "Like what?"

"A couple of AR-15 semi-automatic rifles, one HK MP7 submachine gun, a P226 pistol, some C-4 explosives and remote detonators, to name a few."

Chase and Trevor's eyes rounded.

"Holy crap. Sounds like we might be in business," Chase said.

Alana shook her head. "Just remember, even if you have weapons and ammunition, there are only the three of you who know how to use them. When Delgado shows up, he's not coming by himself."

Carson cracked his knuckles. "We can handle a few more."

"How about thirty or forty more?" Alana said.

"And remember, you're in a tourist town," Lana said. "When the bullets start flying, there will be civilian casualties."

"Lots of bullets means lots more injured." Gina raised her hands. "Just sayin'."

Chase crossed his arms over his chest, a frown pulling his brow low. "The more I think about it, the more convinced I am that I need to go alone and unarmed."

"Or, not at all." Alana crossed to stand in front of him. "You don't stand a chance of coming out of it alive."

He curved a hand around the back of her neck. "Would you miss me if I didn't come back?"

She narrowed her eyes. "You haven't even given me a chance to secure a life insurance policy on my new husband. I can't let you die now."

His mouth curved. "And here I thought you might be remembering why you married me last night."

"Actually, I do remember," she whispered.

"Yeah?" He tipped her face up to his, ready to kiss her when she finally admitted she'd loved making love to him.

Her lips twitched on the corners. "I did it to piss off my father."

Gina laughed out loud. "That's rich. Chase, you don't know her father. I fully expected him to be here by now to drag her ass back to the States, where he'd stand behind her ex-fiancé with a shotgun or a lawyer to see that wedding through."

Chase frowned. "Is that true? You married me to piss off your father?"

She stepped away, lifting her chin. "Why else would I marry a stranger I barely knew?"

Was that it? Had Alana married him to get back at her father? A hard knot settled in Chase's gut. Deep down, he'd hoped she'd married him because she might have fallen in love with him.

Who was he kidding? Only fools fell in love at first sight. Fools like him.

CHAPTER 8

ALANA HELD her pose for as long as she could, determined not to give in and tell the truth. She *had* remembered why she'd married Chase. The night was coming back to her in bits and pieces. The kiss at the wedding chapel had been the catalyst that had opened the door to get her memories flowing. Hearing the bartender and Chase describe the scene at La Casa Loca had brought those memories to life, crowding back into her mind in a jumble of sights, sounds and sensations.

Making love with Chase in the wee hours of the morning had been icing on the wedding cake. She'd loved every minute of it and wished she could relive it all—except for the altercation with Raul Delgado of the Jalisco cartel.

The man had sidled up to her as soon as Chase had ducked out to find a restroom.

She'd ignored Delgado's approach and concentrated her attention on the drink in her hand.

When Delgado had grabbed her arm and forced her to look at him, she'd been shocked by the strength in his grip and his insistence that she go with him.

She'd struggled to free her arm from his grip, but the wiry man was strong, and he hadn't been willing to take no for an answer.

Then Chase had swept in to rescue her, jerking Delgado back by the collar.

The fight that ensued had been a nightmare of flying fists, with every one of Delgado's men wanting a bit of the action.

Chase had pummeled Delgado while fighting off Delgado's minions. He'd stopped one guy from pulling a handgun by knocking it free of his hand with a well-placed sidekick, sending it flying across the floor. Thankfully, the gun had been impossible to find in the darkness of the dimly lit bar.

When he'd subdued eight cartel thugs, including Delgado, Chase had grabbed her hand and led her out of the bar. They'd jumped into the first cab they could flag down on the street and had him drop them a couple of blocks from their resort.

From there, they'd walked the three blocks to the rear entrance of the hotel, keeping to the shadows until they were safely inside and on their way to the third floor, laughing all the way up the staircase. When they'd reached Chase's room, he'd lifted her in his arms and carried her across the threshold, kicking the door closed behind them.

Yeah, she remembered.

Everything.

Down to the number of times she'd called out his name and the way he'd brought her body alive with one orgasm after another.

She'd loved everything about his lovemaking. He'd been concerned about her wants and needs before slaking his own desires. The man had been absolutely right about knowing what a woman wanted. He'd known exactly where to touch her, how much pressure to apply and how long to extend that pleasure before seeking his own.

All these thoughts and feelings rushed back at her like a tsunami, threatening to overwhelm her and drag her under. The depth of her longing for this man scared the living daylights out of her.

So, she did the only thing she could. She pushed him away. Maybe, if he didn't feel obligated to defend her, he would give up on the idea of meeting Delgado on his own, unarmed.

"I'll fix this for both of us," she said. "I'll go back to the States on the next plane out. Then you won't have to meet Delgado and his thugs. They won't be able to use the threat of hurting me to make sure you show up. No one gets hurt, and you can go on with your vacation."

Chase gripped her arm. "Whether or not you leave, I'll still have to deal with the cartel leader. He'll come after me unless I leave."

"Then leave." Alana touched a hand to his chest. "Leave with me. We can take the next plane out of Cabo San Lucas. The two of us. Together."

"You'd do that?" He stared down at her, his hands cupping her elbows. "You'd come with me?"

She nodded. "You bet. Let's pack our bags and get the hell out of Cabo."

"What about getting that annulment?" he asked.

"What annulment?" Trevor asked. "You can't be serious about annulling your marriage already, can you? Damn, Chase, you moved fast. I told you that you needed to get a life, marry and settle down, but I thought you'd take a little more time than one day to find and marry someone."

Chase stared down into Alana's eyes. "Maybe the heart knows more than the head sometimes." He couldn't believe he'd said those words, but once they'd left his mouth, he knew the truth of them.

Alana stared up into his eyes, without blinking. And she didn't refute his statement. She'd come a long way in her thinking about their insane marriage since that morning. Something had changed in her attitude and demeanor at the wedding chapel. Had it been the kiss?

For Chase, it had definitely been the kiss. Their connection had loosened the hold the alcohol had placed on his memories and let them run free again, flooding back into his mind to relive the magic of the evening before. And it had been magical. From dancing a sexy salsa, to saying I do at the little wedding chapel, to making love to his new wife until nearly dawn.

"We'd hate to see you leave and miss the beach and fishing," Trevor said. "But it might be for the best if you both got the hell out of here."

Alana nodded.

"Okay then." Chase clapped his hands together. "Let's get our stuff and get to the airport. We can make flight arrangements there."

Alana spun and headed for her room.

Chase followed.

Alana stuffed her red dress into the suitcase and hurried into the bathroom for her toiletries.

"You okay with this?" Chase asked.

"I wouldn't have offered to leave with you if I weren't," she called out from the bathroom and then emerged with her toiletries kit in hand. She jammed it into her suitcase and zipped it.

Chase stuffed his shaving kit into his duffel bag and hefted it onto his shoulder. "Ready?"

She nodded. "I am."

They headed back into the living room.

"I think it's the right thing to do," Gina said.

"I hate that you're leaving me so soon. Are you sure you're up to facing your father?"

"I wasn't the one to walk out on the wedding," Alana said. "If my father doesn't understand that, I'll keep moving. It's about time I left his house and his corporation and went out on my own."

"I wouldn't be surprised if he busted a gasket when you left the church before he realized what you were going to do," Gina said. "I'm sure he was hot when the best man read Vance's note out loud to all the guests."

"I just couldn't stay and face all of them again. It was too humiliating retreating down the aisle in full white tulle and satin," Alana said.

"Wait," Trevor said, shaking his head. "What church? The one you two got married in last night?"

"No, the one she didn't get married in back in Hawaii," Chase said. "I'll fill you in another time. Right now, we need to get to the airport before it's too late to book a flight out today."

Trevor chuckled. "Like I said, I can't take you anywhere without you causing some kind of trouble."

Chase frowned at his friend. "I don't cause the trouble."

"The bar in San Diego two years ago?" Trevor reminded him.

"I didn't know the woman was married," Chase said. "She didn't wear a ring, and she didn't tell me that little detail."

"What woman?" Alana asked, her eyes narrowed.

"A woman whose name I don't remember." He slipped his hand around her elbow and guided her toward the door, anxious to get her out of the resort before Delgado showed up, and before Trevor spilled all the sordid details of his past romantic escapades. "She doesn't matter. What matters is getting you to the airport and out of Mexico before Delgado has a chance to figure out we're making a run for it."

Stopping short of the door, Alana looked up into Chase's eyes. "Do you think he'll follow us there and shoot up the airplane? I couldn't live with myself if other people were caught in the crossfire."

The concern in Alana's gaze made Chase's heart squeeze tightly. He'd do anything to keep her safe. He hoped he could do just that. Cartel members could be all over Cabo San Lucas. For all they knew, Delgado already had people stationed at the international airport. They'd have to go in wearing disguises, much like they had when they'd visited La Casa Loca.

"I wouldn't put it past Delgado to start a war at the airport," Carson said. "He's really bad news. Only last week, he hung five members of an opposing gang from a bridge at the southern end of Cabo."

Alana shivered. "Now, I'm even more convinced I wasn't meant to come to Cabo. I should've known it was tempting fate to go on a honeymoon without a groom. I've had nothing but bad luck since Vance ran out on me."

"I hope you don't think everything that's happened was bad luck," Chase said. He, for one, was glad she'd come to Cabo. For a die-hard bachelor, meeting Alana had been nothing short of a miracle. She liked to dance, was fun at a party, cared about people and kissed like nobody's business. Making love with her had been unforgettable once he'd remembered every detail of the night before.

"He's right, Alana." Gina reached for Carson's hand. "If you hadn't come to Cabo, you wouldn't have met Chase, had the party of your life, gotten married and had sex with one hunky SEAL. And I wouldn't have met Carson." She lifted her face to the man and batted her eyes.

Carson growled hungrily and dropped a kiss on her lips. "That's right. We wouldn't have crossed paths if you hadn't come to Cabo when you did. I've been considering moving back to the States for a while. Had you and Gina waited much longer, we wouldn't have met. Now, Hawaii's looking really tempting to me."

Gina kissed Carson. "Alana, I think Chase is much better for you than Vanishing Vance."

"I'm not looking forward to going back to Maui and facing my father," Alana said. "He'll find a way to make this all my fault. He thought Vance hung the moon."

Gina snorted. "You'll just have to convince him that Chase is the right man for you."

Alana tilted her head, frowning. "Why would I do that? We're getting an annulment."

Once again, her words struck Chase in the gut. The more time he spent with Alana, the more time he wanted to spend with the woman who was dead set on ending their marriage.

"That might take longer if you don't stay in Mexico to take care of it," Gina pointed out.

Chase almost smiled at Gina's words. Maybe going to Hawaii before the annulment would buy him more time with his reluctant bride.

Alana grimaced. "On the other hand, I won't need an annulment if I'm dead."

Chase frowned, his gut clenching at the thought. His jaw hardened. "We're not giving Delgado that option. Ready?"

Alana nodded and stood back while Chase opened the door.

"Alana, girl!" a deep, familiar voice boomed from the hallway. "You don't know how hard you were to find." An older man with a shock of graying-blond hair and a shadow of a beard stepped through the doorframe. Another man, possibly a bodyguard, in a dark suit and sunglasses waited in the hallway.

Alana ground to a halt, and her jaw dropped. Her father wrapped her in a giant bear hug.

"Daddy?" she said. The single word came out barely above a whisper and then strengthened into a demand. "What are you doing here?"

The older man paused inside the suite and stared around at the others with one eyebrow cocked. Then he turned to face Alana. "I came to bring you back to Maui. I've spoken to Vance. He sends his regrets and is ready to go through with the wedding."

"Are you kidding me?" Alana crossed her arms over her chest. "I wouldn't marry Vance if he were the last man on earth. He cheated on me, Daddy. Did he tell you that?"

"All men can be led astray at different points in their lives," her father said. "Vance just got an earlier start than most."

"I'm not going back to Maui." Alana scooted closer to Chase. "And I'm not marrying Vanishing Vance. That's over. I never should've agreed to marry him in the first place. We weren't meant to be together."

"You agreed to marry him. He's ready to go through with the ceremony to live up to his side of the promise."

Anger burned in Alana. She loved her father, but he could be obtuse and obstinate at the same time. "He broke that promise for good when he didn't show up for the wedding, because he was too tired from boinking the wedding planner."

"That's over," her father said with a dismissive wave of his hand. "He's waiting for you to come back. We can hire a JP to perform the ceremony and have you off on the honeymoon of your choice by the end of the day."

"Daddy…" Alana cupped her father's cheeks between her palms. "I love you, but I'm not marrying Vance. In fact, I'm already married."

"What?" Her father's cheeks burned a bright red, the color extending all the way out to the tips of his ears. "What the hell?" He glanced at the occupants of the room. "Will someone tell me what she's talking about?"

Alana held up her left hand. The one with the plain wedding band on her ring finger. "I got married last night. It's too late for me to marry Vance, even if I wanted to. Which I don't. He's not the man for me."

"But how?" Her father looked around at the faces in the room. "How did you know this person you married? You were set to marry Vance yesterday. It doesn't make any sense."

"It made sense to me. Didn't you marry Mama after knowing her for only three days?"

Her father's frown deepened. "That was different. We didn't have two nickels to rub together."

"I don't have much more than that," Alana said. "And what difference does it make? Sometimes, your heart knows what your head is afraid to admit." She hooked her arm through Chase's. "Daddy, this is my…husband…Chase Flannigan."

Her father glared at Chase, then shot an equally wilting glance at his daughter. "Please tell me this is some kind of joke."

Alana lifted her chin and met her father's glare head-on. "No, this is not a joke. We have the marriage certificate to prove it."

"How can you be married to this man when you were engaged to marry Vance?" her father demanded.

"Daddy, you aren't listening. My engagement to Vance ended the moment he decided to run off with the wedding planner and leave me waiting at the altar."

"I was there. *You* didn't make it to the altar. Who knows, Vance could've shown up, had you walked all the way down the aisle and waited for him. As it is, he's come to his senses and has agreed to fulfill the promise he made to marry you."

"Ha! He was nowhere around. How much more pathetic would I have been had I continued down the aisles and stood there waiting for a groom that obviously wasn't coming?" Alana snorted. "I wouldn't marry Vance now if he were the last man on earth. Besides, like I said, I'm already married." She tightened her hold on Chase's arm. "To this man. Chase, this is my father, Dwayne Neal."

"Nice to meet you, sir." Chase held out his hand.

Alana's father ignored the hand and addressed her. "Do you even know this man?"

"I do. He's a former Navy SEAL. He's going to work in Montana for a protection service. He loves to dance, and so do I. And he's great in bed." She squared her shoulders. "And he would never skip out on me with a wedding planner. He's an honorable man who has vowed to protect me with his own life, unlike Vance. What more do I need to know?"

Chase's heart swelled at Alana's words. He knew she was saying them to stand up to her father, but maybe there was some truth in her words. So, she thought he was great in bed? The corners of his lips quirked. He fought to keep from grinning.

"Don't be ridiculous," Mr. Neal said. "You cannot have married a man in less than twenty-four hours after meeting him. He's a fortune hunter. A gold-digger. Well, I won't have it." Her father even stomped his patent-leather-clad foot in anger. "My attorneys will have the marriage annulled."

"We've already consummated the marriage," Alana said, her cheeks heating slightly.

"Then my lawyers will draw up the papers for your divorce. I will not have you married to someone I don't approve of."

"And how can you disapprove of a man you don't know, Daddy?" Alana planted her hands on her hips.

Damn, she was cute when she was angry.

"Everything I've learned about Chase is good. He served our country, defended our way of life and left the military honorably. He's a good man," she said. "What has Vance done to prove his worth, other than have a high-paying job—a job his father gave him in the business that his father built? Vance never had to work hard for what he has. How does that make him a better man than Chase?" Alana gave her father one of his own looks, staring down her nose at him. "It doesn't. Chase is a better man than Vance could ever hope to be."

"You go, sister," Gina said, and received a

killer look from Alana's father. "Really, Mr. Neal, Alana wouldn't have been happy with Vance. You don't want your daughter to marry a man who doesn't make her happy, do you?"

Alana's father didn't look at Gina. His gaze remained locked on his daughter. "I don't want any man to marry you for my money." His gaze shifted to Chase, and his eyes narrowed. "I'll give my money to charity before I let it go to someone who marries my daughter to get to my fortune."

Chase's body stiffened next to Alana. "Is that what this is all about? You think I married your daughter to get to your money?" He laughed, the sound jarring on Alana's ears. "I don't know who you are, or how much money you're worth. Nor do I care. I have enough of my own. Money I saved while on active duty, defending your right to make as much money as you want. Defending *your way* of life. I put my life on the line for you, Alana and every American because it's what I believe in. I don't want your money. I have my own—money I earned with my blood, sweat and a few tears along the way. I hope to use that money to buy a small ranch in Montana. It won't be much, but it'll be enough. Enough to live on, to raise a few horses and cows and, maybe, a family. I have an honorable job awaiting me in Montana. One that will allow me to provide for your daughter and any children that might come along. What more do I need?"

Alana smiled, her eyes glistening. "Nothing." She'd only ever wanted a place to call her own. A place she could get to know the neighbors and establish relationships with people who didn't work for her father.

"Hell, Chase," Gina said. "You make me wish you'd chosen me."

"Hey," Carson cut in. "He's married."

"Right." Gina grinned. "He's married to my best friend, and I couldn't be happier for them."

"And right now, Chase and I are headed to the airport to return to the States," Alana said. "If you'll excuse us, we'll be on our way."

"Why are you headed to the States?" her father asked, his expression sour. "If you just married, I would've thought you'd stick around here to enjoy your honeymoon."

Alana scrambled for an excuse that didn't involve telling her father she had a death threat out on her, and Chase was certain to be killed if he met with the cartel leader. "Uh... We've decided we'd prefer to spend our honeymoon in Montana. I much prefer the mountains to getting sand in my shorts."

"I'm not done with you, young lady." Her father stepped in front of her, blocking her path. His bodyguard remained in the hallway, on alert and ready to assist.

"Daddy, I'm twenty-eight years old. I don't need your permission to do what I want. If I want pepperoni on my pizza, I'll have pepperoni on my pizza."

Her father stared at her as if she'd lost her mind. "What in the fool-darn-hell are you talking about?"

"I'm going. And there's nothing you can do to stop me." Dragging her suitcase behind her, Alana dodged her father and headed for the elevator.

Chase started to pass Mr. Neal when the man shifted to stand in front of him. This wasn't the best first impression a man could make on his father-in-law, but he couldn't worry about it now. Not when Alana was still in danger.

Mr. Neal poked a finger into Chase's chest. "If you so much as make my daughter cry, I'll hire a hit man and put you out of her misery. Do you understand?"

Chase didn't bother to tell Mr. Neal that all of Alana's protestations were bogus and that she planned to ditch him as soon as it was humanly possible. Annulment, divorce, whatever it took, she planned to untie the knot they'd forged with tequila and good times on the beaches of Cabo.

He couldn't blame her or her father for their skepticism. If he had a daughter, he'd be livid if she married a guy after knowing him for only a few hours. He'd be worried like Alana's father that he'd married her for other than honorable reasons.

"Sir, I can assure you I'm not after your money. Your daughter is special. She's a beautiful woman who deserves to love whomever she wants. But she also deserves someone who respects her and treats her right. I can promise you, I would never hurt your daughter. I only want to protect her. Now, if you'll excuse me, I'm going with my wife." He pushed past Mr. Neal and joined Alana at the elevator just as the bell rang and the doors slid open. He'd just promised Alana's father he'd protect her. Hell, he'd already promised himself that he would. Now, he had to live up to that promise.

As he stepped into the elevator, he heard a shout from the hallway. "Hey, wait up."

When the doors started to close, Chase pushed the button to keep them open long enough for Trevor to slide through. Then he turned and held the doors for Carson.

Trevor let go of the door and grinned. "We thought you might need backup getting to the airport."

Carson grimaced as he punched the button for the ground level. "I feel kind of sorry for the ladies we left with Alana's father."

"Me, too," Alana said. "He'll be grilling Gina about now." Her lips curled upward at the corners. "She'll give him hell. She loves pushing all of his buttons."

"I love when she pushes all of mine," Carson said. "That's one sassy female." He clapped his hands together. "Just the way I like them."

Alana frowned. "Don't you hurt my friend."

Carson held up his hands. "I wouldn't dare. Besides, she scares me." He chuckled. "I haven't felt this alive since I came down to Cabo San Lucas. I didn't realize how much I missed all the action and danger associated with being a Navy SEAL." He turned to Chase. "I don't suppose your boss in Montana could use another SEAL on his team, could he?"

"It doesn't hurt to ask. All he can say is no." Chase slipped an arm around Alana's waist and pulled her close. "Remind me to give you his phone number."

Carson nodded. "Will do."

When they reached the ground floor, the doors slid open, and the three men escorted Alana to the concierge's desk, where she requested a taxicab to take them to the airport.

As they waited inside the lobby for the taxi to arrive, Chase kept a vigilant eye on the people coming and going. If anyone looked the least bit suspicious, he'd be ready to throw himself in front of Alana to protect her from harm.

Nothing happened, and soon one of the hotel valets came through the door and motioned for them to come. "Your taxi has arrived."

Chase slipped his arm around Alana again and pressed his body close to hers, providing a shield of flesh and bone to protect her against bullets, knives or other forms of attack.

The hairs on the back of his neck stood at attention as he walked out of the lobby. Carson and Trevor were his wingmen, also providing a human shield to protect Alana.

A taxicab idled at the curb. The hotel valet hurried forward to open the door for her.

Glancing first left and then right, Chase motioned for Alana to slide in first.

Trevor rounded the back of the vehicle to the other side.

Carson stood at the trunk, ready to toss the luggage inside as soon as the driver popped the latch.

Chase lifted his foot to slide into the vehicle beside Alana.

A pop erupted behind Chase, followed by a stinging sensation in his back and a crackling sound. Electricity ripped through him.

His muscles locked, frozen in mid-step. He couldn't grip the door, his hands useless. His jaw clamped so hard it hurt.

Move, he urged himself.

Nothing.

Not even a finger responded. He couldn't control his breathing.

A crackling sound filled his ears like the snapping of his bones from the inside out.

Chase's vision jolted, the world tilted and gravity took him down. He crashed into the pavement. With no way to catch himself, his shoulder hit first, pain shooting through him. His cheek slammed against the asphalt.

An engine revved, and tires squealed. As the taxi leaped forward, the door slammed shut.

Chase lay twitching, helpless and trapped in a body that wouldn't work as he watched the taxi streak away.

"Fuck!" Carson yelled.

"Chase," Trevor dropped down beside him. "What happened? Are you okay?"

He couldn't respond. Nothing worked but his mind. Even that was confused and off-kilter.

The crackling stopped.

Air slammed back into his lungs. He drew in a ragged gasp.

One clear thought emerged in his rattled brain.

Alana. Have to get to Alana.

He willed his body to move. Muscles spasmed, but they were too weak—dead weight.

The taxi disappeared around a corner.

Too late.

The cab was gone.

"Chase, what the hell?" Trevor leaned over

him, studying his body, his gaze narrowing. "Oh, shit. Carson," he yelled, "someone nailed him with a taser."

Carson and the valet raced past Chase and Trevor, disappearing out of Chase's range.

Trevor reached behind Chase and yanked on something that amplified the stinging sensation that had started the whole incident.

Chase groaned.

"Can you move?" Trevor asked.

"Not," Chase managed to move his fingers, "much." He stared up into Trevor's eyes. "Alana?"

Trevor shook his head, his lips forming a thin line. "Carson couldn't get into the cab fast enough. You went down before I knew what was happening and... she's gone."

Chase tried to rise, his body feeling like it weighed a ton. "Son of a bitch!"

This was not the plan he'd envisioned. He should have been with Alana.

"What do we do now?" Trevor asked.

"Get me up," Chase grunted.

Trevor slipped an arm beneath Chase's shoulders.

Carson appeared on Chase's other side,

breathing hard. "Whoever fired the taser is long gone."

"As is Alana," Chase said through gritted teeth.

Between Carson and Trevor, Chase rose from the ground, his legs twitching, the muscles not quite ready to hold him.

His friends half-carried him into the hotel. With each step, his muscles and resolve strengthened. By the time the elevator reached his floor, he could manage on his own.

The elevator dinged, the door slid open and Chase stepped out and strode toward Alana's room, where her father waited.

"What's the plan?" Trevor asked.

His jaw hardened. "Either I'll meet with Delgado at midnight, or we come up with a better plan."

CHAPTER 9

As soon as the vehicle took off, Alana knew she was in trouble.

"Chase!" she cried out. With the sudden goosing of the accelerator, the open door to the back seat slammed shut. She reached for the door handle and pulled hard, but it wouldn't open. The child locks had been activated. The only way she could get out was if someone opened the door from the outside.

She spun in her seat and looked back, praying Chase and his friends could somehow stop the vehicle and free her. She froze.

Chase lay still on the ground as the cab shot forward, moving faster and faster. He'd been about to get in the car when he'd dropped. Was he injured or worse... she gulped... dead?

Despair fell like lead to the pit of Alana's belly. All their planning to get out of the country went up in the smoke of the burned rubber from the tires spinning across the pavement. She had no doubt she was on the way to Raul Delgado, the leader of the Jalisco cartel.

Sure, she was afraid for her own life, but now that she was a prisoner, she knew Chase would come after her. He'd be tortured and killed, possibly like the men who'd been hanged from the bridge a week before.

Alana couldn't let that happen. In the short time she'd known Chase, she'd discovered a decent human being. A man others should be more like. A man who would selflessly defend his country and those weaker than himself. He'd come for her and put himself at risk.

Chase had faced untold horrors and risks as a Navy SEAL. He deserved to enjoy his life now that he was out of the military. She couldn't let him risk everything to save her. She had to find a way out of this mess before Chase met Delgado at the proposed deadline.

The particular cab she was in was more modern than most. Alana searched the interior for a weapon, anything she could use to crack a window or the unbreakable Plexiglass barrier between the front and back seats. She couldn't reach around to grab the driver by the neck and force him to stop, but she had to get out of the vehicle before she was delivered to the cartel leader. Once in his hands, she'd be surrounded by far too many of his minions to make an escape. Escape had to be now or never.

Banging against the shield between her and the driver did nothing to slow the vehicle. Alana kicked at the window, knowing her soft-soled shoes wouldn't be effective, but she had to try. She dug in her purse for anything she could use to break the glass, but all she could find was a pen and an emery board, neither of which was strong enough to break through the glass. She tried sliding the emery board down between the window and the door to trigger the locking mechanism. When the driver took a turn too sharply, Alana lost her grip on the emery board, which slipped out of her hand and fell inside the door. She tried ripping the door apart but only managed to break her fingernails. The seat had been cleaned of all objects. Not even an umbrella existed inside the confines of the back seat.

When all her efforts failed, Alana turned in

her seat and looked out the back window at the disappearing resort hotel. With no cell phone, she couldn't call and tell them which way they were headed, and she couldn't use the hard case of the cell phone to help her break the window. She was stuck and on her way to meet a killer.

The cab weaved between the streets and alleys, leaving the more affluent neighborhoods of timeshare condos and vacation homes, and headed into the outlying areas of tin-roofed shacks and concrete-block buildings with laundry hanging from clotheslines and windows. The farther they went from the beach, the deeper into despair Alana sank.

How could Chase find her? He would be left with no other choice but to show up when Delgado demanded. The problem was, even if he did show up, Delgado probably wouldn't let her go in exchange for Chase's cooperation. He'd have Chase and no other reason to keep her alive. He'd certainly make an example of Chase to his men and everyone else in Cabo.

Her heart beat fast, and her chest hurt at the thought of Raul Delgado hanging Chase from a bridge. She couldn't let that happen. *Wouldn't* let it happen. Somehow, she had to get away before midnight and let Chase know he didn't have to meet with Delgado. She'd find her way back to the airport, they'd catch the next flight back to the States and she and Chase would live happily ever after.

And pigs would learn to fly.

The cab weaved through narrow streets and roads, climbing into the hills surrounding Cabo San Lucas. Soon, they turned into a gated compound surrounded by high stucco walls. Armed guards stood on either side of the vehicle. The driver spoke to them in Spanish. One of them relayed a message via a hand-held radio. The staticky response came back, and the gate opened. The driver pulled into the compound, and the gate slid shut behind them.

Alana studied the fence, the gate and the surrounding grounds, committing everything she could see to memory. If—no, *when* she escaped, she would have to navigate the grounds in the dark. How she'd get over the seven-foot walls, she wasn't certain, but she'd cross that hurdle once she was free of her confinement.

The vehicle came to a halt in front of a sweeping, white marble staircase leading up to rich mahogany double doors.

The doors opened, and several men, armed with what looked like military-grade rifles, emerged and surrounded the vehicle.

Alana forced calm to her hammering heart. She couldn't show fear. To escape her current situation, she had to use her head. Cowering in terror would get her nowhere.

The door opened, and a man reached inside, grabbed her arm and dragged her out onto the brick paving stones of the driveway.

"Let go of me, you Neanderthal." Alana jerked her arm free and straightened.

Laughter sounded from the top of the stairs. A Hispanic man dressed in white trousers, a black button-up shirt and sunglasses looked down on her. He was surrounded by four men dressed in black, wearing sunglasses, radio headsets in their ears and carrying more military-style rifles.

The man at the center nodded to the men surrounding the taxi. He spoke quickly in Spanish. *"Tráeme a la mujer,"* he commanded.

The man she'd shaken loose from grabbed her arm. When she struggled to be free, another man gripped her other arm. Together, they half-dragged, half-carried her up the stairs to stand in front of the man in the tailored, white trousers.

All Alana could think of was how much she wanted to bloody those white trousers. The man had to be Delgado—a dangerous man, full of his own sense of self-worth, bent on retribution for being bested in front of his men.

Alana glared at the man who'd terrorized entire cities and preyed on innocents. Carson had told her of how Delgado would steal young girls and sell them into the sex trade, and how his thugs made millions trafficking drugs and humans across the border into the United States. She had no respect for this man, especially when he wanted to make an example out of her husband.

To hell with that.

Alana vowed to get out of Delgado's compound as soon as possible. She just had to play along and pretend to be a poor, weak female who didn't have a brain in her head. Then, perhaps, he'd think she was too dumb and wimpy to find a way out of captivity.

"You are the gringo's *esposa,*" he said and touched a hand to her hair. "*Tú eres una mujer bonita.* Beautiful." He captured strands of her blond hair between his fingers and rubbed them as if testing the texture.

Alana longed to slap his hand away and wipe the smirk off his face, but instead, she let her poker face fall into place, masking any emotion the man could use against her. She'd learned to play poker from her father. He was a master of poker faces and had taught her the secrets of bluffing from a very young age. Her father had made a killing in the oil speculation business by keeping his emotions in check and making the best possible deals through patience and cunning.

If Alana hoped to get out of Delgado's compound alive, she had to use her mind. Though she was physically fit, she was no match for the superior strength of Delgado's male entourage.

"Your *esposo* will be at La Casa Loca tonight. He will not want anything to happen to his pretty bride." He clasped her chin in his grip and turned her face up to his. "But once I'm done with him, *tú me perteneces*. You will be mine."

Alana bit down hard on her tongue to keep from telling the man to go to hell.

Delgado jerked his head. *"Encerrarla en la bodega."*

The men holding her arms carried her up the steps and into the house. They passed through a grand entryway and through a dining room. All the way, Alana studied her surroundings, memorizing the number of steps, the doors and windows she could see. The place was opulent, decorated with rich mahogany furniture, expensive Persian rugs and original paintings on the walls.

The men carried her into a large kitchen with ultra-modern appliances and wide granite countertops. A windowed door led off the kitchen to the outside. But it wasn't through that door that she was carried.

Another door opened onto a wooden staircase leading down into a darkened cellar with rack after rack filled with bottles of wine. At the back of the wine cellar was another wooden door, shorter, stouter and hinged with iron.

Alana shivered in apprehension.

The men were headed straight for that little door. As they neared, Alana struggled to free her arms, bucking and kicking with all of her strength.

The men were much stronger than she was. No matter how hard she tried, she couldn't work herself free. They only tightened their hold on her until she was certain they would break her arms. She'd have bruises where they'd held her.

One man lifted a metal latch, opened the door, and together, the two men shoved her inside.

As soon as she got her feet beneath her, she scrambled toward the door and pushed against it.

She was too late. The door closed, the latch slid into place and she was trapped in a dark, cool cell beneath a killer's lair.

"Where's my daughter?" Dwayne Neal asked as soon as Chase, Trevor and Carson entered the hotel room without Alana.

"Have a seat, Mr. Neal," Chase said.

"I will not sit. I demand to know what you've done with Alana." He stood his ground, his face a mottled red, his brow deeply furrowed. "Where's my daughter?"

"Oh, my God." Gina's eyes filled with tears,

and she walked into Carson's arms. "He got her, didn't he?"

Chase nodded. "The cab driver took off with Alana before any of us could get into the vehicle with her." He pulled his phone out of his pocket, preparing to dial the only man he could think of who could help.

"What are you talking about?" Mr. Neal asked. "Why did the cab driver take off with her? Where did he take her? Who has my daughter?" He stalked across the room, grabbed Chase by the collar and got in his face. "I want answers. Now!"

Chase held stock-still. He understood the man's rage. He deserved it. "Mr. Neal, your daughter has most likely been taken by Raul Delgado, the leader of the Jalisco cartel here in Cabo."

"The leader of a cartel has my daughter?" Mr. Neal's face grew redder. "You said you'd protect my daughter. How's that working out for you? My daughter could be killed because of your incompetence."

Chase couldn't refute the man's accusation. He felt the same way. If he'd gotten in first, he wouldn't have been hit by the taser, and he'd at least have had a chance of saving Alana. Now, he had no idea where they were taking her or what they'd do to her. His chest was so tight, it hurt. "Excuse me, sir," He pushed past Mr. Neal and hurried to the bedroom where Alana had slept, closing the door behind him.

He hit the phone number for Hank Patterson, praying he'd already come up with a solution to his problem.

Hank's phone rang and rang. He didn't answer. Chase stared at the phone.

Out of options and with no help coming, Chase couldn't stand around and feel sorry for himself. It wasn't his way. He had to take action. If they had only three Navy SEALs, they had to come up with a solution involving just the three of them.

A knock on the door made him stop in the middle of pacing the floor.

Gina pushed the door open and stuck her head inside. "We need a plan."

"I know," Chase said.

"Any ideas?" she asked.

He nodded, a plan starting to form, but it depended on information they didn't have. "We need to find where Delgado lives. I bet that's where he's taken Alana. If we can find him quickly, we take the fight to him."

"I'm in," Gina said. "I can fire an AR-15. I qualified on an M4A1 rifle in Army Basic Combat Training. I shot expert every time we qualified. That brings our number up to four."

"Against potentially one hundred cartel members?" He shook his head. "It's a suicide mission."

"Yeah, but you can't go it alone," she said.

"No," Trevor pushed through the door, "you can't go it alone. So, you'll have to take us along with you. Carson left a few minutes ago."

A stab of disappointment ripped through Chase. He'd thought the Navy SEAL would stand with them.

Trevor grinned. "Carson went to check with his contacts. They should have a good idea of where to find Delgado. As soon as he gets the information we need, he'll be back to take us to his place to pick up the contraband weapons he's stockpiled."

A wave of hope washed over Chase. Since seeing the cab drive off with Alana inside, he hadn't been sure he'd ever see her again. But with the help of his fellow SEALs, he began to think it might be possible. "Whatever we do, it has to be at Delgado's place, not at La Casa Loca. I can't imagine he's taking Alana to the bar. He probably has her locked up at his place. We have the rest of the day and into the evening to make this mission happen."

"God, I hope Alana is all right," Gina said. "I can't imagine how she felt being kidnapped and driven away by one of Delgado's thugs. She has to be terrified."

Chase knew how it felt to lie in the street, helplessly watching the woman he'd married on a whim being driven away to God knew where. It felt like crap. He'd failed her completely. All his focus now was on getting her back. Whatever he had to do, even if it meant giving himself into the hands of a murderous cartel leader, so be it.

Dwayne Neal pushed through the door into Alana's room. He poked a finger into Chase's chest. "This is all your fault. What the hell did you do to piss off the leader of a god damn cartel?"

"I defended her when Delgado tried to leave the bar with her."

"Defended her?" Mr. Neal's anger was plain

to see in the ruddy red his face had turned. "How did you defend her?"

"I threw a few punches. Apparently, I humiliated him in front of his men, and if I don't show up at La Casa Loca at midnight, he'll kill Alana."

Neal's brow dipped low, his eyes narrowing. "If he tried to leave the bar with her before, what makes you think he'll let her go if you show up?" Neal asked.

"That's just it," Chase said. "We don't think he'll release her."

"Mr. Neal, if Chase meets with Delgado, the cartel leader will have all his gang members there," Gina said.

"They'll kill him," Alana's father said. "Not that I'm against that. However, will that get Alana back?"

"It won't," Chase said. "That's why we have to come up with a better plan."

"And what is that plan?" Mr. Neal demanded.

"We go to Delgado's compound and get Alana before the midnight deadline."

"And how do you propose to do that?" Neal asked.

Chase lifted his chin toward the door. "First, we have to find out where he lives. Carson just left to tap into his contacts for information on the location of Delgado's compound. We'll form a plan once we know more."

"If they know Alana is my daughter," Mr. Neal said, "perhaps they'll negotiate a ransom for her."

"I'm not sure they know she's the daughter of a wealthy man," Chase said.

Mr. Neal pulled his cell phone out of his pocket. "I'm willing to pay a ransom to get my daughter back safely."

Chase held up his hand. "If they don't know she's worth a huge ransom, let's not complicate the situation by giving them that information. Delgado is known for human trafficking. If he kills me, he won't kill Alana."

"He'll do much worse," Gina said, her voice flat, her face strained. "We have to get to her first."

"Then what are we waiting for?" Mr. Neal asked.

"Like I said—information. As soon as Carson gets back to us, we'll make a plan and implement."

Mr. Neal snorted. "I'm not a patient man."

"Yes, sir," Chase said. "But we can't rescue her until we know where she is. Until then, we wait."

Mr. Neal's eyes narrowed. "Understand this," he said. "My daughter and I don't always see eye to eye. But she's all the family I have. I love her and will do anything in my power to get her back. Alive."

"Understood," Chase said. "And you should know that even though we haven't known each other long, I have great respect and feelings for Alana. I will move heaven and earth to bring her back alive."

Chase held Mr. Neal's gaze for several long seconds before the old man nodded.

Her father lifted his chin. "Once we get her back, I'm taking her home to Maui."

"I won't stand in your way," Chase said. "If that's what she wants."

Mr. Neal opened his mouth as if he wanted to say more. Instead, he closed his mouth and returned to the sitting room.

Waiting, for Carson, proved to be painfully tense.

Mr. Neal paced the sitting room of the suite alongside Chase. Alana's father called every one of his own contacts in Mexico, searching for someone who could help. No one offered assistance against the Jalisco cartel. The US State Department offered to look into the matter if Mr. Neal would go to the consular agent in San José del Cabo and file an official request. Mr. Neal told them what they could do with their request, hung up and resumed pacing.

On a couple of occasions, Mr. Neal and Chase almost ran into each other. When that happened, Alana's father would glare and mutter something to the effect of Chase having failed his daughter, and what was she thinking getting involved with a washed-up SEAL?

Chase held his tongue, determined to conserve energy for the fight ahead. If Delgado had an army of cartel supporters behind him, it could be a bloody battle in which he and his friends might end up dead. And if that happened, what would Delgado do with Alana?

Chase refused to consider that as an option. Whatever he and his friends did, they had to get Alana out of Delgado's hands and back to her father. Until he had her somewhere safe, Chase couldn't leave Mexico for the wilds of Montana. Hank would wait for him to come to work for the Brotherhood Protectors. He was a reasonable man with a wife and children. He'd understand Chase's desire to protect his own wife and bring her back to a safe and secure location. If it meant taking on an entire army of cartel members, Hank would do it for his family. Chase would do no less for his wife.

Despite the fact he'd only just met the woman he'd married, he liked her. Hell, he'd broken all his self-imposed rules about never marrying for this woman after just a few hours with her. He would never consider leaving her at the mercy of a dangerous man like Raul Delgado.

In the meantime, he waited for Carson to return with word on where to find Delgado and, hopefully, Alana.

Minutes later, a knock at the suite door heralded the return of Carson with the news he'd been waiting for. Alana's father stood beside Chase as Carson, the resident former SEAL of Cabo San Lucas, shared what little information he'd been able to attain.

"Delgado lives in a compound west of town," Carson said. He pulled a piece of notebook paper from his back pocket, unfolded it and spread it out on a table. Someone had drawn an image of Cabo with the main roads noted and an arrow pointing to a location northeast of town.

Carson pointed to the location. "Delgado has a compound with walls seven feet high. The guy I spoke with has been inside the compound. He helped to build it and knows all the places Delgado could have stashed Alana. He thinks Delgado will have incarcerated her in the wine cellar. There's a small storage closet at the back of the cellar with a lock on the outside of the door."

Chase's fist clenched. The only reason to have a lock on the outside of a door was to imprison whoever was on the inside. When he got hold of Delgado, he'd make him pay for taking Alana and subjecting her to being imprisoned in some dark, dank cellar.

"Okay." Chase drew in a deep breath and looked up into Carson's eyes. "Now that we know where Delgado's compound is, we'll need your stash of weapons."

Carson met his gaze. "You know, going up against the cartel is suicide, don't you?"

Chase nodded. "I can't leave her there, and we can't shoot up a bar full of innocent people."

A slow grin spread across Carson's face. "I was beginning to go crazy here with so much sun, sand and relaxation." He clapped his hands together. "I'm ready for action."

Chase's heart skipped several beats and then thrummed a steady, strong tattoo. Calm determination spread through him like it had with every mission he'd undertaken as a Navy SEAL. "Let's do this."

ALANA STOOD IN THE DARK, praying her eyes would adjust to the limited lighting. However, the lighting wasn't just limited; it was nonexistent. Once she came to that conclusion, she felt her way around her prison, seeing with her hands everything in the room besides herself, and hoping the cell didn't contain any other living creatures. The possibility of finding spiders, rats and mice made her shiver. But if the cell contained rats or mice, it might have a gap or hole, something she could widen and dig out enough to fit through. She refused to give up hope of escaping.

The cell contained a pail and nothing else. But the floor was made of dirt like the rest of the wine cellar. She supposed the pail was for relieving herself. But she refused to believe she'd be in the cell long enough to need it. If anything, she'd use the pail to dig into the dirt floor. Maybe she could tunnel beneath the wall back into the wine cellar.

Since no one knew where Delgado had taken her, she was on her own. She couldn't sit around and wait for anyone to rescue her. She had to do something to get herself out of her current situation.

Using the bucket, she dug into the hard-packed earth and scraped away a thin layer of dirt. She felt the ground, despair threatening to overwhelm her. She'd barely made a dent in the earthen floor.

Now wasn't the time to give up. Alana stiffened her resolve and dug in. A little at a time, she expanded the impression until it was as deep as her fist. Her hands hurt, and her arms and back began to ache. But, she couldn't stop now. The longer she took, the closer the hour drew to Chase's meeting with Delgado at La Casa Loca. She had to find a way out and get to Chase before he walked into certain death with Delgado and his armed-to-the-teeth cartel thugs.

She didn't know how long she'd been trapped in the cell. With no light from the sun to gauge the time of day, she could only guess at the number of hours that had passed. It felt like forever, but she supposed it was getting to be late afternoon. Evening would be upon them soon, and so far, no one had come down to check on her, nor had they offered her water or food. Why should they? And if anyone did come down, what would she do? The potential scenarios made her shiver in the cool dampness of the cellar prison.

She'd never been this frightened in her life. Nor had she been this determined. If she could keep her focus on escape, she wouldn't succumb to complete despair.

Footsteps sounded outside the door of her cell, and the sound of metal scraping across metal alerted Alana that someone was opening the door.

She dropped to the dirt floor and played dead, her hand on the bucket, her body tense as she readied to spring into action.

The dull yellow light from the wine cellar spilled into her cell.

"*Señora?*" a male voice said.

Alana lay on the ground and moaned softly,

but loud enough for the man standing outside her door to hear.

A plastic bottle of water landed on the ground beside her, but the man didn't enter.

When the door started to close, Alana ramped up the sick act and moaned louder. If he didn't fall for it, she might lose her only chance to get out of the cell.

The door stopped closing, leaving a wedge of light crossing over her face. The wedge broadened as the door opened wider.

"*Señora?*" the man called out, the sound closer this time.

He stepped into the cell and nudged her foot with the toe of his shoe. "*¿Estás bien?*"

From beneath her lashes, Alana studied the man. Dressed all in black, his arms covered in tattoos, the man carried a rifle and smelled of sweat.

She moaned again and pulled her legs in, balling her body into the fetal position.

The man squatted beside her and touched the barrel of his rifle to her temple. "Bang," he said softly.

Anger surged through Alana at the man's sadistic taunt. Her hand closed around the rim of the pail, and she brought it up hard and fast, aiming for the man's face.

The pail caught him on the nose, and the crunch of cartilage echoed off the walls.

His hand flew to his face. Blood spewed from his nose, and he swung the rifle away from Alana's head.

This was her chance, her only opportunity. Alana had to move. With her legs cocked already, she kicked out both feet, catching the man in the knees. He fell backward, landing hard on his ass.

Alana scrambled to her feet and dove for the door.

The man roared behind her and lunged after her.

She made it through first and slammed the door, but the man's hands were in the way.

He screamed and withdrew his hands, giving Alana a second shot at closing the cell door. This time, she succeeded, dropping the bar into place and locking the man inside.

She didn't have much time. Once he figured out he was locked in, he'd probably start shooting the rifle at the door. The bullets would splinter the wood. If he had enough ammunition, he'd break through and get out.

Not to mention, the sound of the gunfire might filter through the building and draw the attention of Delgado's goons.

Alana raced through the racks of wine to the stairs leading up into the kitchen. Once at the top, she paused long enough to ease open the door and peer out. Two men stood in the kitchen, each armed with a rifle. One drank from a water bottle.

The other said something in Spanish that made the water bottle guy laugh.

A sound from the other end of the kitchen made them look up.

A man in a white smock entered and spoke sharply to the two men with guns.

The men snorted and talked back to the man in the white smock, but they left the kitchen soon after.

Alana assumed the man in the white smock was the cook. He pulled pots from a rack beside the gas stove about the same time as the guard in the cellar started firing his rifle. Though the sound was muffled by the walls of the basement, Alana held her breath.

If the cook heard the muffled sound of gunfire, he might alert the men he'd just chased out of his kitchen. Alana had to get out of there before they discovered she'd escaped her cell.

The cook filled a pot with water and set it on the stove. He switched on the overhead vent, the sound filling the kitchen with enough noise that Alana hoped it would mask the sound of the gunfire below.

Then the cook turned toward her hideout and crossed the kitchen.

Alana shrank back against the wall at the top of the stairs and waited for the cook to push the basement door fully open.

When a few seconds passed, and that didn't happen, she peered out. Another door stood open beside the cellar door. The kitchen stood empty. The cook was in a closet or pantry beside the cellar door, and the path was clear from where she stood at the top of the cellar steps to the exit door that led from the kitchen to the outside.

Alana dragged in a deep breath and made a break for it. She ran lightly through the kitchen, her focus on the door to the outside. Her heart pounded, her pulse pushing blood and adrenaline through her system. She was only a few steps away from freedom.

As she reached for the doorknob, a shout

sounded behind her. Alana froze and turned back to the man on the other side of the kitchen.

The cook had come out of the pantry, carrying a canister and a couple of bottles of spices. He frowned fiercely and spoke to her in rapid Spanish.

She shook her head. *"No comprendo."* Alana eased backward toward the door, pressing a finger to her lips. *"Por favor,"* she said, having exhausted her memory of the Spanish she'd taken in school. *"Por favor."*

The muffled sound of gunfire sounded again from the basement.

The cook's gaze shifted to the basement door, his eyes narrowing. When the sound of wood splintering and a shout rose from below, the cook looked to her, his eyes widening. He gave her a chin lift and whispered, *"Darse prisa."* With his hands full, all he could do was jerk his head toward the outside door.

Alana nearly cried with her relief. *"Gracias, mi amigo."*

"Go. *Desapareces.*"

Footsteps sounded on the staircase from the cellar.

Alana turned and ran out the door into the shadowed dusk.

THE BAND of four former military members gathered at Carson's small house on the beach. Inside, in a secret room hidden in one of the stucco walls, Chase, Gina and Trevor discovered an arsenal of weaponry.

Chase had chosen to carry an AR-15 rifle with a scope. For backup, he tucked a 9mm P226 into a shoulder holster he wore beneath a light black jacket.

Thankfully, Carson had a stash of black clothing they used to camouflage themselves in the night. The former SEAL even offered camo sticks for them to use to blacken their faces.

"Are you sure you can handle that weapon?" Carson asked Gina.

She nodded, hefting the AR-15 in her hands. "I've got this."

He handed her a magazine and a box of bullets. "What was your MOS in the Army?"

She glanced away. "Doesn't matter. They train everyone in basic combat skills. I qualified as an expert marksman. That's all you need to know." She filled the magazine with rounds and slammed it into the weapon. "I'm ready to go."

"You think Mr. Neal will stay put in the hotel room until we get back to him?" Trevor asked.

Gina shrugged. "We can only hope."

Carson grunted. "I read him the riot act about getting in the way of anything we're doing to rescue Alana. He understands we're up against some pretty bad dudes."

"Does he also understand that you three are highly trained Navy SEALs?" Gina asked.

"I explained it to him. He wanted to come with us, but I told him he needed to stay at the hotel in case Alana was freed and made her way back. She'd be frightened and would need someone she knew and loved to be there for her."

Gina nodded. "That ought to do it."

"I also told him that if he interfered with our mission, I'd shoot him," Carson said.

"I'm glad you told him that and not me," Chase admitted. "That man is my father-in-law. Shooting him wouldn't make my new bride happy."

"Speaking of which," Trevor said. "What the hell made you tie the knot in the first place?"

"A lot of tequila and a special woman who loves life and has a good heart," Chase said. "Now, let's go get her back, or my marriage will set records for how short it was."

"You thinking of staying married?" Trevor asked. "If I recall correctly, you always swore you'd stay a bachelor for life."

"Things change," Chase said, his answer short, almost terse. He didn't want to waste time explaining himself when he wasn't all that sure of why he'd married Alana in the first place. The argument *because it felt right* seemed lame, though it was true. Whatever the reason, he had to save Alana from Delgado, or none of his reasons would matter.

As they were loading into Carson's SUV, Chase's cellphone buzzed in his pocket. He dug it out. UNKNOWN CALLER displayed on the screen. Thinking it might be Delgado, he hit the talk button. "Yeah."

"Flannigan? Hank, here."

"Hank, we're about to head out. Do you have any suggestions on how to handle this situation?"

"Yeah, wait for us," Hank said.

"What do you mean?" Chase stared out at the lengthening shadows. "I can't wait. We're taking the fight to Delgado at his place in the hills outside of the city. If we don't leave now, we might not catch him at home."

"Then go but send me the GPS location. We're at the airport, loading into vehicles as we speak."

"You're here?" Chase's heart swelled with hope. "In Cabo San Lucas?"

"We are." Hank chuckled. "Me and five of my best men. Send us the location. We'll join you as soon as we can."

Chase sent Delgado's address to Hank in a text and then asked, "What about arms?"

"We arrived in a private plane. We have what we need," Hank said. "Don't wait on us. If you can slow them down long enough for us to get there, we might even the odds a little." Hank paused. "Any word on the girl? Have you located her?"

"No on both counts. All we have is Delgado's deadline. Midnight tonight. If the preemptive attack doesn't work out, I'll fall back on the original demand," his gut knotted, "and pray the bastard doesn't change his mind and kill Alana first."

"Right," Hank said. "We're on our way."

Trevor stood at Chase's side as he ended the call. "Was that Hank?"

Chase nodded. "I can't believe he made it here in just a few hours."

"Here in Cabo?"

"Yup," Chase said. "With five of his best men."

Trevor grinned. "That's Hank for you. He's there when you need him. And he has a network of friends with money and assets who can get him where he needs to be, when he needs to get there." Trevor clapped his hands together. "Gang, we have backup. This mission's odds just got better."

Chase wasn't as quick to think everything would turn out roses. "We still don't have a bead on Alana. She might not even be in Delgado's compound. He could've taken her to some other cartel location."

"From what my sources tell me, Delgado likes to run his operation out of his house. He has it set up the way he likes, and the high wall around it slows down or keeps out the riffraff."

"Speaking of which," Gina said, "we'll have to scale that wall. I was never good at vertical leaps, and I'm barely five and a half feet tall."

"We've scaled walls in Iraq and Afghanistan," Trevor said.

"We've got this," Carson said. "And we'll get you over it. No worries."

"Good," Gina said. "Then maybe we'd better get going so we can get into place before sundown."

"Shouldn't we wait for Hank and his men?" Carson asked.

Chase shook his head. "I'm afraid that if we wait too long, there might not be anything left of Alana. He has the address and GPS. He'll be here in time to provide the backup we'll need. In the meantime, we can scope the surroundings and come up with a plan to breach the compound. Hopefully, Hank and his guys will get there before we're in so far over our heads we can't dig our way out."

Carson chose a 9mm Glock and stuffed explosives into one of his pockets and detonators in the other. "Let's get moving."

Gina and the three former Navy SEALs piled into Carson's SUV and headed out of the city and up into the hills overlooking Cabo and the ocean in the distance. The sun was just slipping into the ocean when they arrived at a location where they could hide the vehicle. At a mile away from their target, they'd continue on foot to the compound and perform a quick reconnaissance of the walls, the security system and take a count of the number of guards on duty. With only the four of them to start with, they could easily be bested in a matter of minutes if discovered. An all-out attack wasn't an option. They had to sneak in by scaling a wall. Then they'd have to take out the exterior guards, enter Delgado's home, locate Alana and get her out without her being harmed. The chances of them getting in, extracting Alana and getting back out without alerting Delgado's men were slim. But they had to find Alana before Delgado used her to force them to lay down their arms and surrender to him and his men. Just like surrendering to the Taliban, the odds of the SEALs surviving once that happened were nil.

Being caught wasn't an option.

From all Carson had told them, the cartel members were ruthless and always out for blood. They didn't let their enemies go unharmed. Most of the time, they used them as examples, torturing and killing them as a warning to others not to cross them. Raul

Delgado was one of the worst for using this terror tactic.

After they hid the truck in the brush, the men and Gina gathered their weapons and took off over the hills, moving in the direction of Delgado's home. They moved quickly across rough terrain, careful not to expose themselves to anyone who might be lurking. The setting sun cast long, dark shadows, giving them sufficient concealment as they navigated the hills and gullies, working their way toward Delgado's compound.

The road curving up to the hilltop hideaway switched back and forth. The four of them kept climbing, keeping a watch on the road from a distance. So far, they hadn't seen anyone going up or down.

Chase worried they were setting their sights on the wrong goal. Alana might not be inside the cartel leader's compound after all. If she wasn't, they would have wasted precious time getting there. However, with no other intel on Delgado's haunts, they didn't have any other choice.

First over the top of the ridge, Chase spotted the compound on the next rise. He stopped and held up a fist for the others to stop as well.

They lined up just below the ridge to look over the rise and study their target.

Surrounded by high walls, the building within them was large and sprawling, with windows on the upper level that probably offered a great view of the ocean below.

"I spot a guard on the rooftop." Carson handed Chase the binoculars he'd brought along with him.

Chase had been looking through the scope of his rifle and had yet to spot him. With the wider range of the binoculars, he quickly located the man dressed in black, carrying a rifle. He leaned against a wall, staring out over the road leading up to the main gate.

Chase looked closer. "Two men on the gate, and one roaming the outer wall on this side. For all we know, there might be another on the other side and the rear."

"We can take out the guy on the wall and go over the top," Trevor said. He glanced at the last of the sun dipping downward into the ocean to the west.

"By the time we get close to the wall, it'll be

dark enough to provide cover for our approach," Gina said.

At that moment, Chase's cell phone vibrated in his pocket. He pulled it out and stared down at the name on the screen. He hit the talk button and pressed the phone to his ear. "Hey, Hank."

"We ran into a bit of luck at the airport," Hank said. "At the general aviation ramp, we overheard the pilot of another plane talking to a truck driver about a delivery he had for the same address as the one you gave us. We waited until he'd loaded the cargo from the plane into the truck. When he had it all loaded, he went back into the terminal, giving us the opportunity to add to his cargo."

"What are you telling me?" Chase asked.

Hank chuckled. "We hitched a ride in the back of the delivery truck. We're well on our way."

Chase could feel the weight of the mission ease a little. "That's good news."

"All we need is for you to make sure we get past whatever guards might be at the gate checking the delivery trucks," Hank said.

"We'll do our best," Chase promised. "Be prepared in case we aren't successful."

"Roger," Hank said and ended the call.

Chase pocketed his cell phone and turned the binoculars on the narrow, winding road leading up to Delgado's compound. "The cavalry is on the way. They hitched a ride in the back of a delivery truck destined for the Delgado compound."

Trevor clapped Chase on his back. "I told you Hank was a standup kind of guy. Trust him to be there when you need him."

"We have to get to the compound before they arrive and neutralize the guards on the gate, so that they don't inspect the back of the delivery truck. At the very least, we need to create enough of a distraction to give the guys a chance to exit the truck and enter the compound on their own."

"I think we can do that," Carson said. "I have the C-4 explosives I brought with me. We can set up a pretty decent distraction on the back side of the compound—enough to take their minds off what's out front."

"Okay, Carson, you're on for setting charges," Chase said. "Make noise, not so much damage. We don't know for sure where inside they might be keeping Alana. We need to time it for when Trevor and I are at the wall. Blow the charge, and we'll go over during the confusion. Once we're inside, we'll find Alana."

Trevor's lips twisted. "That's a tall order for three SEALs and a soldier."

Chase shrugged. "Sometimes, less is better. We have less chance of being discovered when there are only two of us on the inside."

"Two? No way. What about me?" Gina asked.

"You need to be Carson's backup while he's setting charges. Once he triggers the explosion, you two can slip around to the front and take out the guards on the gate. Since we don't have radios, we'll communicate via cell phone texts and coordinate our efforts that way. But first, we need to get to the base of the compound. Set your phones to silent if you haven't already."

Chase checked through the binoculars again and spotted the headlights of a vehicle on the road, climbing up the hill from far below. He trained the lenses on it. When it switched back, he could tell it was a cargo truck. "We need to get moving. Hank and his team are on their way up now and will be here soon. We need to be ready when they arrive. I anticipate no more than ten minutes."

"Let's do this," Trevor said.

Carson grinned in the dusk, his teeth flashing white in the darkening gloom. "God, I missed this."

"Just don't do anything to put yourself or others at any more risk than we'll already have," Chase warned. "Our number one goal is to get Alana out alive."

Carson gave a mock salute. "Gotcha."

"Will do," Trevor said.

"Operation Save Alana," Gina said. "But, boy, I want to kick some Delgado ass while we're at it."

"We might get our chance," Chase said. "Let's just make sure he doesn't end up kicking ours or Alana's first."

ALANA MADE it outside the kitchen only to find herself in a driveway that led around the side of the sprawling house. Dusk was settling in around the house, but the stars had yet to make their appearance in the sky to light her path. She clung to the shadows of the mansion, though the white stucco would probably silhouette her body against it. She bent low and moved close to the bushes and small trees planted close to the building.

Her heart hammered in her chest, but she couldn't let fear rule her. She'd come this far; she wouldn't let them recapture her and take her back to Delgado. He might grow tired of dealing with her and kill her outright. Without her, he wouldn't have a bargaining chip to lure

Chase to his assignation at La Casa Loca. Then again, Chase wouldn't know she was dead and would show up anyway. He wouldn't give up on her if he thought there was any chance of saving her from Delgado.

No, she had to stay alive, get the hell off the compound and find her way back to Cabo San Lucas to stop Chase from showing up at midnight.

As she approached a corner, she heard men's voices. She dropped to her haunches beside a yucca plant and froze.

A shout sounded behind her, and a man burst through the door of the kitchen she'd come out of moments before.

Alana swore beneath her breath. She recognized the man she'd hit over the head with the bucket and locked in the cell below. She shrank lower in the shadows and prayed he wouldn't see her.

Two other men rounded the corner she'd almost gone around and ran toward the shouting man. They spoke in rapid Spanish.

While they were occupied, Alana crawled behind the yucca plant on her hands and knees to the corner of the building, took a deep breath and slipped around it. Then she scrambled to her feet and ran for the compound wall. Her pulse beat so hard against her eardrums she could barely hear anything else. She made it to the wall, and no one was shouting. No footsteps sounded behind her. But there was nothing to climb to get over the top. She moved amongst the bushes along the wall until she reached a trellis covered in bougainvillea vines and blossoms.

Heart pounding and breathing ragged, she dug her feet into the trellis and climbed, her hands and face scraped by the branches. After she'd made it only four feet up the trellis, hands gripped her around her hips and jerked her from her perch and back to the ground.

Alana dropped to her hands and knees, rolled onto her back and leveled a kick at the man's groin.

He cursed in Spanish and doubled over, giving Alana time to crab-crawl backward. She flipped over and launched herself away from the man, only to run headfirst into another. This one caught her around her middle and crushed her against him, pinning her arms to her sides. She couldn't get enough leverage to kick him hard, and she couldn't wiggle her way free. He held onto her so tightly that she could barely breathe.

The man spoke in Spanish to someone else and then carried her, kicking and writhing, to the front of the house, where he tossed her to the ground.

Alana rolled and sprang to her feet, ready to run. One glance around made her freeze in place.

Lights shone down on her from the corners of the house. Four men pointed rifles at her, their fingers on the triggers, ready to shoot.

Raul Delgado emerged from the house and descended the steps to where she stood, a handgun pointed at her chest. "Go. Run for it. I have no use for you. You have caused enough trouble."

"You want me to run so you can shoot me in the back." She squared her shoulders and lifted her chin. "If you're going to shoot me, do it now. I want you to look into the eyes of the woman you're about to kill."

Delgado's eyes narrowed. He raised his handgun, pointing it at Alana's face. "It would be a shame to destroy such a pretty face." He lowered the weapon, and his lips curled into a sneer. "I have much better use for one like you."

He nodded toward the man closest to him. "Tie her up and put her in my bedroom. And when I'm done with you," he leaned close to Alana's face and sneered, "my men can have you to do with as they will."

Alana's stomach roiled. These men were animals. She'd die before she let one of them rape her—especially Delgado. As the man approached her, she bunched her muscles, ready to fight with every last breath.

CHASE AND TREVOR positioned themselves at one side of the compound while Carson and Gina worked their way around to the back. Up until they were within a couple of yards of the compound, Chase had kept an eye on the guard on the roof. That man's attention seemed to be on the front of the house and the road leading up to the compound. The truck headlights were within a quarter mile of the gate and closing fast.

Chase's cell phone vibrated in his pocket. He pulled it out, cupped his hands around the screen and read the text.

Carson: Ready

He texted back.

Chase: Go

A loud explosion erupted.

Trevor bent and cupped his hands.

Chase stepped into them and reached for the top of the wall. He dragged himself up to the top and lay low until he was sure all was clear. The guard on the roof had moved to the rear of the building to check out what had caused the explosion.

Chase reached down, grabbed Trevor's hand and helped him scale the wall. Once they were both on top, Chase slipped over the side and dropped to the ground.

Men shouted nearby.

Chase focused on his main goal—find Alana. "Go help Carson and Gina secure the gate. I'll look for Alana."

"You need someone on your six."

"I can move better alone," Chase said. "And they need the help. The sooner Hank and his guys get inside, the better off we'll be."

Trevor nodded. "On it." He ducked into the shadows and moved around the side of the house toward the front.

Alone, Chase tried to think like Delgado. If he had Alana here, where would he keep her? Chase was about to slip in through some

French doors when his cell phone vibrated in his pocket.

He dug it out, hid in the shadow of a bush, cupped his hand around the glowing screen and read the message. His breath caught in his throat, and his heart skipped several beats. The message was from Trevor.

Trevor: She's out front

His gut instinct was to run around to where Trevor was and confront whoever had Alana. Thankfully, reason followed close behind instinct, giving him pause. If Alana was out front, someone held her prisoner or at gunpoint. He could do nothing to help her if they shot her in front of him. Delgado would know this and demand he throw down his weapons and give himself up.

Chase squelched his urge to confront Delgado and entered the house through the French doors. He hurried through what appeared to be a study with bookshelves lining the walls. As he came to the front foyer, he spied a man carrying a submachine gun heading up a staircase. Chase watched as he cleared the landing above and ran to the end of what sounded like a hallway. Based on the pounding of footsteps, the man raced up more steps.

Chase checked all directions and then ran up the staircase to the second floor. He turned the direction the other man had gone and found another set of steps at the end of a hallway. These steps were narrower and appeared to lead to the roof.

Easing up the steps, he rose to the top of the building where the roof had been turned into a patio. Two men stood looking over the edge of the stucco wall down to the ground in front of the house.

Chase emerged onto the patio and crept forward, one quiet step at a time.

Shouts from below captured the guards' attention and held it.

Walking stealthily, Chase closed the distance between him and the two men. When he reached them, he grabbed both of their heads and smashed them together as hard as he could. Neither man saw him coming and, apparently, hadn't expected to be attacked on the rooftop. Too stunned to fire, they staggered. One fell to his knees and toppled over. The other reeled and lifted his weapon. Before he could fire, Chase hit him in the side of his head with the butt of his weapon.

The second man dropped to the ground, out cold.

Chase peered over the side of the patio to the front of the house, where Raul Delgado stood in the light shining out from the front entrance. He held Alana in a headlock, a handgun pointed at her temple. Four of his men stood around him, weapons at the ready.

Beyond the front of the house, the driveway curved through manicured gardens to the gate, not visible from where Delgado stood. The delivery truck sat in the gateway with no guards in sight.

Shadows slipped along the inside wall of the compound.

Hope stirred inside Chase.

Hank and his team had arrived and breached the compound's walls.

Chase hoped they weren't too late to keep Delgado from killing Alana. His jaw set in a firm line, he balanced his rifle on the edge of the patio wall and aimed at Delgado's head. The man was far too close to Alana. If Chase got a clear shot, he'd take it. However, with Delgado's other men lined up around him, he might only have time to kill Delgado. The others could turn their weapons on Alana and take her down before Chase or the rest of the team could do anything about it.

Delgado spoke to his men in short, clipped tones. All but two of them turned outward, and the others moved closer to Delgado, using their bodies as shields to protect their boss.

One of the two men at Chase's feet stirred. Chase slammed the butt of his weapon onto the man's head and returned his attention to the drama unfolding in front of him.

"What is your husband's name?" Delgado demanded of Alana.

"I'm not married," she replied.

Delgado tightened his hold on her neck. "Tell me his name, or I'll kill you now."

Alana's cheeks turned red, then purple.

Chase nearly climbed over the edge of the wall and dropped down onto Delgado. His body burned with the heat of his anger.

"Joe Smith," Alana choked out. "His name is Joe Smith."

Delgado loosened his hold enough that she could breathe again. "You are lying. But you better hope he comes." Then he turned toward the gate. "Chase Flannigan," he called out.

"Come forward now, or I'll kill your pretty wife."

"He's not here," Alana said. "And he's not my husband, I tell you. He won't come for me. He has no reason to." Her voice was gravelly and shook with each word. Still, she stuck to her story and refused to confirm Chase's name. Hell, she had no reason to believe he would come for her. She likely thought he didn't have any way to find her.

His heart squeezed hard in his chest. The woman stood bravely in the face of a murderer. His estimation of her grew even more. He'd known she was feisty by her reaction when she'd woken up after their crazy night. She'd been bound and determined to set things right.

Now surrounded by men who could easily rape or kill her, she dared to defy them. Chase wished he could spare her this nightmare. He was the one Delgado wanted. Yet, Alana was the one bearing the brunt of the cartel leader's anger.

As much as Chase wanted to go down and challenge Delgado face-to-face, he was in the right position to take him out. All he needed was an opportunity. If only Alana could lean her head forward or slide downward.

Delgado raised the barrel of his pistol and fired a round into the air. "The next one goes into her, unless you come forward."

A hand on Chase's arm made him jump.

"Go," Trevor whispered. "I'll take the shot. Try to get her to duck."

Knowing Trevor was even a better shot than he was, Chase relinquished his position and backed away from the edge. Afraid Delgado would make good on his promise to kill Alana, Chase ran down the stairs and out through the front entrance of the house.

"Don't shoot," Chase called out. He held up the rifle he'd brought with him and raised his other hand in surrender. "Please, don't shoot her. Let her go and take me. It's me you want anyway."

Delgado's men shifted their aim to dead-center on Chase's chest. But Delgado didn't lower the barrel of his pistol from Alana's temple. "You have dishonored me in front of my men. For this, you will pay."

"Then let me pay. Let the woman go free." Chase met Alana's gaze and held it.

Alana gave him a sad smile. "You shouldn't have come. He'll kill me anyway."

"Not if I can help it. I wouldn't have you

hurt, no matter if you *ducked* out on me," he said, praying she'd get the hint from the emphasis on one word.

Alana frowned. "I didn't duck out on you. Delgado's driver took off with me."

"Delgado is an animal," Chase said, widening his eyes as he willed her to understand his coded messages. "A duck who quacks too much."

"Enough of your words," Delgado demanded. "Throw down your weapon now."

"You made a pass at my wife in that bar and refused to back down. I did what any husband would do and defended my wife." Chase lifted his chin and glared at Delgado. "As far as I'm concerned, you got what you deserved."

"This is my country." Delgado tightened his hold on Alana's neck. "I do as I please." The cartel leader drew the gun away from Alana's temple and pointed it at Chase. "And it pleases me to kill you."

Alana jabbed her elbow into Delgado's ribs.

Chase sucked in a breath and ducked, sure he would be shot.

Delgado's hand jerked. The weapon went off, the shot going wide of the target, catching one of his own men's right arm. The man cursed, dropped his gun and slapped a hand over his wound.

Delgado's hold loosened on Alana's neck.

She slammed her fist into his crotch. "That is my husband you're talking about, and I'm not ready to call it quits on him," she said through gritted teeth. "I've barely gotten to know him."

Delgado hunched over, giving Alana enough room to duck under his arm, grab the wrist of the hand holding the gun and yank it up behind his back. "Now, tell your men to lay down their weapons."

Chase's chest swelled with pride at how fierce Alana was with Delgado.

Delgado clamped his jaw shut, refusing to give the order.

Alana pushed his arm up higher between his shoulder blades. She plucked the pistol from his grip and held it to Delgado's leg. "Tell them, or I'll shoot first one leg, and then the other."

The cartel leader grunted. His face broke out in a sweat and turned a ruddy red. Finally, he spoke in Spanish.

His men didn't budge, but held onto their weapons, pointing them at Chase.

"I get the feeling you didn't do as I said." Still holding the arm up between his shoulder blades, she pressed the pistol into his thigh. "Think I won't pull the trigger? Remember who was going to rape me and then turn me over to his men to do with as they pleased?" She shifted the barrel of the pistol and pulled the trigger, hitting the tip of Delgado's toe.

The man screamed and would have hopped up and down, but Alana had his arm in her grip and refused to ease up on the pressure she applied.

"The leg is next," she warned him.

Chase chuckled. "If there's one thing I've learned about my wife, she's a very determined woman. I'd do as she says."

"Exactly," Hank Patterson stepped out of the shadows, carrying a submachine gun. "Your men are surrounded. Have them put down their weapons."

"Now," Chase said, his voice steely. He'd had it with Delgado and his threats. "I have a man on the roof, ready to shoot you as soon as my wife is done with you."

Delgado glared at Chase and muttered Spanish obscenities beneath his breath. Then he took a deep breath and shouted to his men.

One by one, they threw down their weapons and held their hands in the air.

Trevor herded the two men down from the roof at gunpoint.

Three of Hank's men collected the guns and knives from Delgado's men and patted them down, finding more on their bodies. When they were divested of their weapons, Hank had his men load them into the back of the delivery truck and lock the door. Hank paid the driver to take them to the south side of Cabo San Lucas and let them loose in their rival gang's territory. That left only Delgado himself.

"We'll take care of Delgado." Hank took over from Alana and zip-tied Delgado's wrists behind his back.

Chase closed the distance between him and Alana and pulled her into his arms.

"There's an extradition order for him, but the Mexican government won't do anything to release him to the US," Trevor said.

"I know someone who could help get him to the US," Carson said. "Let me handle it."

"Who is it?" Hank asked.

"The less you know, the better," Carson said. "My friend doesn't always follow the rules."

"Hank, this is Carson," Chase said. "Former Navy SEAL."

"Thought I recognized you." Hank held out his hand. "We served a deployment together." His eyes narrowed. "I think it was in Iraq." He shook his head. "I'm pretty sure you saved my ass on that mission. It's been a while."

Carson grasped Hank's hand. "I think it was the other way around. You saved my ass."

Hank waved a hand at the men standing around. "How did you end up helping Trevor and Chase?"

With a shrug, Carson said, "I've been an expatriate for several months here in Cabo."

"Well, if you decide you've had too much fun in the sun," Hank said, "the demand is greater than the supply of Brotherhood Protectors. You're welcome to join Brotherhood Protectors in Montana or one of my other locations across the US." He tilted his head, his eyes narrowing. "Or you could join my newest acquisition, the Stealth Operations Specialists. That might be right up your alley."

Carson shot a grin toward Gina. "I'll consider it. Working this mission reminded me of all the fun I've been missing."

"Well, the offer is open," Hank said.

"In the meantime, I'll take out the trash," Carson tipped his chin toward Delgado. "Should I dump him in the ocean and save time and tax dollars on his extradition?"

"I don't really care what you do with him," Chase said, "as long as he doesn't bother Alana ever again."

"If he's wanted Stateside," Hank said, "and you can get him there, take him."

Carson nodded. "I spotted a sweet Ferrari 296 GTB parked in a garage on the south side of the compound. Raul and I will go for a little ride. Then I'll hand him off to my friend who will get him where he needs to go."

"Can you handle him by yourself?" Hank asked. "I can send one of my men with you as backup."

Carson shook his head. "I've got this. If he gives me any trouble," he touched the barrel of his handgun to Delgado's temple, "I'll take care of him. The world would be a better place with one less murderous cartel leader. Hang onto him. I'll be back in a minute." Carson left them with the cartel leader.

Raul glared at Chase and Alana. "The rest of my men will come. They will kill all of you."

"I suspect you have them positioned at the

La Casa Loca for our midnight rendezvous," Chase said. "We'll just send word to that location that their leader has been extradited to the US, and the rest of your team from the compound will be landing in the rival cartel's turf. I'm sure they'll head that way to help their brothers out, or fade into the shadows since their leadership has been compromised."

"You won't get me out of Mexico. They'll stop you before that happens," Delgado said.

"Are you sure?" Alana tilted her head. "Do you see any of your men standing in our way?" She shook her head. "No. You're on your way out."

The roar of a high-performance engine sounded as a bright red low-slung Ferrari rounded the corner of the mansion, skidding sideways. It came to a stop a few feet from Delgado.

Hank and Swede marched him to the passenger side of the vehicle, shoved him in and slammed the door shut.

"Good luck," Hank called out to Carson.

Carson revved the engine and shot out of the compound, speeding away into the night.

Alana leaned into Chase's embrace and rested her cheek against his chest. "I didn't think you'd come after me. I thought you wouldn't find me."

"As you might've noticed, Carson has connections. That's how we found Delgado's place. We took a risk and bet everything on Delgado taking you to his compound." He held her close. "Thank God we were right."

She pressed her face into his shirt, her body shaking against his. "I was trying to get loose, so you wouldn't have to save me. I almost made it."

Chase chuckled. "Sweetheart, you did a good job saving yourself. I have no doubt you'd have gotten free without our help."

"I'm not so sure," Alana said. "But I wasn't going to go down without a fight."

"That's my girl." Chase kissed the top of her head. "Brave and feisty. I love that about you."

"Where did you come up with all these people?" she asked and pushed away far enough to look at the men gathered around her and Chase.

"This is my new boss, Hank Patterson, the founder of the Brotherhood Protectors." Chase held out his hand to Hank. "Thanks for coming so fast."

"Glad to help." Hank turned to the others in

his group. "Guys, you know Trevor Anderson already. And this is the newest member of the brotherhood, Chase Flannigan. I knew him as Salty Dog when we served together." Hank pointed to a tall man with broad shoulders and blond hair. "This is Swede, he's our computer guy." Hank nodded to the next guys and went down the line. "Meet Taz, Viper, Maddog and Boomer. Fortunately, they were able to cut loose long enough to come down and help out on this job. You'll meet the rest of the Brotherhood Protectors team when you get to Montana." He nodded toward Alana and smiled. "And you must be the reason for our mission. Do I get a formal introduction?"

"This is Alana, my wife." Chase's arm tightened around her, and he pressed another kiss to the top of her head. "One of the bravest people I've ever met."

Hank grinned. "I saw how you handled Delgado. If you ever decide to go into the protective service, I might have a place for you in the Brotherhood Protectors."

Alana laughed. "Thanks, but I think I'll stick to something less intense." She leaned into Chase. "Although I will be job hunting now that I've decided to quit my father's firm. I'm skilled in scuba diving and large corporation management, not that I want to continue down that path." She shrugged. "But that's for another day. I'm just glad to have survived tonight. Thank you all for coming to my rescue."

Chase turned to the others. "Hank, this is Gina, Alana's friend," he said, reaching out to pat her shoulder. "She's prior Army.

Hank shook Gina's hand. "Good to meet you. Thank you for joining the mission."

Gina nodded. "It was my pleasure.

Hank turned toward Chase. "Let's get out of here before any more of Delgado's men come looking for him." He faced Chase. "Are you ready to leave paradise and come to Montana? If so, I have an airplane waiting to take us home."

Chase stared down into Alana's eyes. "I just got here. As long as Delgado's people aren't gunning for me, I'd like to finish my vacation before I start work."

Alana met his gaze, a smile curving the corners of her lips.

Gina leaned close to Alana. "You need to get in touch with your father as soon as possible. I'll bet he's contacted the Mexican government, the US Embassy and the French Foreign Legion by now."

Alana's smile slipped. "He'll want me to go back to Maui immediately."

"You don't have to go, you know," Gina pointed out. "Carson said he'd take care of Delgado. I have no doubt he'll make that happen. The man has some wicked connections."

"I would like to stay," Alana said. "We didn't come all this way to turn around and go home after only two days."

"I'll be here all week," Chase said. "I could use a good dance partner."

Gina nudged Alana with an elbow. "You hear that? How can you pass up an opportunity like that? The man can dance. And it will give you all week to figure out how to annul the marriage…" Gina winked. "Or not."

"I promised Lana she'd get to put her toes in the sand. I'm staying," Trevor said. "I'll be here as backup."

Chase cupped Alana's cheek. "What do you say? Want to hang out on the beach for the rest of the week?" He held his breath, hoping. After all they'd been through, he wanted to get to know this amazing woman better.

Alana glanced down at the ring on her finger. She touched his hand with the ring on it and finally looked up. "I don't want to go back to the Maui yet. I'd like to get to know Cabo a little better, as well as a certain groom, who apparently swept me off my feet in a few short hours. Do you suppose we could take it slow… and sober?"

"What? And take all the fun out of it?" Gina laughed. "You really do need to loosen up, Alana. You only live once. Take a chance."

Chase lifted her hand to his lips and pressed a kiss into her palm. "We can go as slow and as sober as you like. I'd like to get to know the bride who made me want to get married when I had no intention of ever doing so." His heart swelled with the hope and joy of getting a second chance with this amazing, brave woman. He hoped the week didn't go by too fast. He wanted more time with Alana than one week would provide. But he'd take all he could get and then work on convincing her to give him more.

THEY RODE BACK to the hotel in Carson's SUV, with Trevor driving since Carson was on the mission to deliver Delgado to his contact, who would take him back to the States to stand trial for a number of crimes. Hopefully, he'd be locked in jail for the rest of his life, without any access to his cartel.

A shiver snaked down Alana's spine. What if Carson had been too cocky about being able to handle the cartel kingpin? What if some of Delgado's men were, at that moment, waiting for Carson and Delgado to show up at the airport?

Seated beside Chase in the back seat of the SUV, Alana leaned into the man who was her husband, at least for now. Gina had called shotgun in the front passenger seat, where she helped Trevor navigate the dark roads out of the hills and back to Cabo San Lucas.

"Will you hear from Carson once he transfers Delgado into his contact's custody?" Alana asked.

Chase took her hand and gave it a gentle squeeze. "He'll notify us as soon as he hands off Delgado." When his cell phone vibrated in his pants pocket, he pulled it out and stared down at the screen. "Speak of the devil. Carson just texted that he made the hand-off. Delgado is on a plane headed for California, where he'll be met by the U.S. Marshals. His contact will text Carson when they complete that hand-off." Chase slipped an arm around Alana's shoulders. "Delgado is officially out of the picture."

"Hooyah!" Trevor called out. "Now, we can get on with our vacation. Lana doesn't need any more stress than she's suffered already. We don't want that baby coming any sooner than its regularly scheduled time." Trevor's gaze reflected in the rearview mirror. "Is Carson meeting us back at the hotel?"

"Not right away," Gina said, her brow puckering. "He wanted to check on the men they're releasing into enemy cartel territory before he comes back."

Trevor shot a glance toward Gina. "In the Ferrari?"

Gina shrugged. "Apparently, the man likes a little drama."

"Then he picked the right girl," Alana said with a smile.

Gina's lips twisted. "What do you mean? I'm low to no drama."

Alana snorted. "You're one kick ass female, which makes you all drama. I'm not sure I could've charged into a cartel compound like you did."

"You were doing a damned fine job of trying to escape," Chase said.

"If you recall," she said, "I didn't quite make it."

Chase brought her hand to his lips. "You were holding your own."

"Long enough for us to get there," Gina added.

"Thankfully, you did get there, along with Hank's team." Alana frowned. "Do you really think the rest of the cartel will leave us alone?"

"Hard to say," Chase's brow dipped. "I've heard of occasions when a cartel leader is murdered, and all hell breaks loose between opposing cartels, all vying for territory."

"Thanks, man," Trevor said, his lips pressing into a tight line. "Makes me want to pack up my pregnant wife and leave as soon as possible."

"I'm sure everything will be fine," Gina said.

Trevor cocked an eyebrow in Gina's direction. "So sure you'd bet my wife and child's lives on it?"

"I'd hate to leave when we've barely begun our vacation," Gina said.

Alana hated to leave when she hadn't had enough time to get to know the man she'd married on a drinking binge. "We need time to figure out our legal situation," Alana said, not wanting to call it an annulment. Not when she might not want to annul her insane wedding to the man sitting beside her. If they left now, she'd be on her way back to Hawaii, and Chase would head for Montana and his new job with Hank Patterson's Brotherhood Protectors. They'd never see each other again.

As her heart squeezed hard in her chest, her fingers tightened in his.

Alana couldn't wait to get back to the hotel and maybe spend some alone time with the man. When they pulled into the parking lot beside the hotel, she remembered why that would not be possible. Her father was there, waiting anxiously for her. He'd likely want to pack her up and take her back to Hawaii, out of harm's way.

She couldn't let him do that. Not when she hadn't figured out what to do about a marriage that never should have happened and a husband she was beginning to realize was everything she could have wished for.

First thing she'd do once she got past her father was get a shower. She'd have to borrow more of Gina's clothes. Then she'd think about food. They hadn't eaten dinner, and her stomach was rumbling in protest. After the basics, she'd think about how somewhere in the past few chaotic hours, she'd stopped thinking of Chase as a stranger and now thought of him as her husband.

Chase's cell phone vibrated in his pocket. He pulled it out and frowned down at the screen. "Fuck," he said. "We've got a problem."

"What?" Alana leaned over in an attempt to read the text message.

"It's Carson," Chase said. "He said he ran into one of the members of the cartel they turned loose. He said that once they'd learned more about Alana Neal and that her father, Dwayne Neal, was rich and in the country, Delgado decided he could kidnap Alana and demand ransom for her. He'd meet with Chase, dispatch him and collect a million dollars for the girl. He sent his second in command with a team to keep an eye on Dwayne Neal and take him if things didn't go according to plan."

Alana froze. "That means, they could be here."

Chase nodded, his gaze going to the hotel and the grounds surrounding it. "By now, they have to have heard about Delgado."

"My father could be in danger." Alana reached for the door handle before Trevor had brought the vehicle to a complete stop. She shoved open the door.

Before she could jump out, Chase grabbed her arm. He had his phone to his ear. "Hank, Dwayne Neal might be in trouble. Delgado's second in command might attempt to take him, if they haven't already." He glanced toward the road leading into the hotel grounds. "Take the front entrance. Trevor, Gina and I will take the back. Alana will be with us."

Trevor turned the SUV sideways in the

driveway that led around to the back of the building, effectively blocking any other vehicle from coming through. He shoved the SUV into park and flung open his door.

Alana shook Chase's hand off his arm.

Chase reached behind his seat for the AR-15 rifle he'd stowed there. Trevor and Gina gathered their weapons and dropped to the ground.

Hank's SUV, filled with the men he'd brought with him from Montana, blew past the side of the hotel and skidded to a halt at the front entrance.

Chase, Alana, Trevor and Gina made their way around the side of the big hotel to the back service entrance, where a large black SUV was backed up at an angle, engine running as if to say, *We won't be here long.*

Two men carrying military-grade rifles burst through the back door into the dull yellow light glowing over the loading dock. Following them were two more men, gripping the arms of a man between them. He wore khaki trousers, a linen blazer and had a black sack pulled over his head. His hands were bound behind his back, and he wasn't going willingly.

"Let me go." The man dug his heels in and twisted in an attempt to shake free of the hands holding him. "You won't get away with this."

Alana gasped. "Daddy. Oh, dear God. That's my father." She lunged forward.

Chase's arm shot out, grabbed her arm and yanked her to the ground behind a border of bushes. She tried to rise, but he held her still.

"Stay down," he ordered quietly. "Promise me you'll stay here."

Alana frowned at the men dragging her father forward.

Chase cupped her cheek. "Promise."

She didn't want to promise when every instinct made her want to rush those men and pummel them into the ground for trying to kidnap her father.

Trevor and Gina dropped down beside them, peering through the bushes at the men manhandling Alana's father.

"We can't let them take him," Alana whispered.

"Agreed." Chase pulled out his cell phone and sent a text. "I notified Hank."

"We can't wait. They're going to load him up," Trevor said.

The cartel men shoved her father toward

the SUV. One of the leading armed men opened the back door.

"I need to get closer," Chase said. "Cover me."

Trevor poked his rifle barrel through a gap in the bushes and nodded. "Got your six."

Chase took off. Hunkering low, he followed the line of bushes to the end, his rifle at the ready.

When they jerked her father roughly toward the open door of the vehicle, the older man dug in his heels. "I'm not going with you. You can't make me go." He threw himself back-ward, landing hard on the pavement, using his weight to anchor him to the ground.

"Daddy, get down!" Alana yelled. "Stay down!"

Her father rolled to the side, away from the men and pressed himself flat against the pavement.

The men holding the rifles turned toward the sound of Alana's voice and raised their weapons. Standing in the light over the loading dock, they probably couldn't see where Alana, Trevor and Gina lay in the dark behind the bushes. Still, Alana lay as flat to the ground as she could get and watched as Chase came at the men from a different direction than the one they were staring at. When he was close enough to get in a clear shot, he dropped to one knee and raised his rifle to his shoulder.

One of the men turned his raised rifle toward Chase.

Alana sucked in a breath and prayed.

The crack of a shot being fired sounded next to Alana.

The man aiming at Chase dropped to the ground, his weapon clattering against the ground.

Chase fired, taking out the other man whose weapon was aimed in Alana's direction.

One of the men who'd been dragging Alana's father lurched for the driver's door.

"The tires," a voice said behind Alana. Hank ran forward and aimed his rifle. "Shoot the tires." He fired a round, hitting the right front tire.

Trevor took out the front left tire.

The man who'd lunged for the driver's door yanked it open. Before he could jump in, Gina sent a bullet through the driver's windshield. The man cursed in Spanish, slammed the door shut and ran hunkered low toward the trees at the far side of the loading area.

The last man standing bent toward the older man on the ground. Before he could lay a hand on him, Chase fired, hitting the man in the shoulder. He stumbled backward, clutching the wound. Once he regained his balance, he staggered toward the tree line and disappeared into the shadows.

Hank's team ran after the two men who'd escaped.

Alana shot up and ran down to the loading dock.

Chase knelt beside her father, pulled the hood off his head and checked for a pulse.

Her father blinked up at the Navy SEAL, his hair and clothing disheveled, a bruise forming on his jaw. "You."

"Yes, sir," Chase said.

Dwayne Neal snorted. "About time you got back. Where's my daughter?"

"I'm here, Daddy." Alana dropped to her knees beside him, her chest tight at the sight of her father lying against the ground, looking like an old man, not the strong, unflappable CEO of his multimillion-dollar corporation. "You okay?"

"I'm fine."

She wrapped her arms around his neck. "I was so afraid for you."

"I'm fine," he said gruffly.

She leaned back and studied his face. "You fell on the pavement."

"It was a strategic decision," he said. "It's one thing to shove an upright man into a car, but quite another to lift two hundred and thirty pounds of dead weight."

"You had me worried," she said.

"I was worried about you," he said, his face softening. "Those men had you. Are you all right? Did they hurt you?"

"I'm okay." She shot a smile toward Chase. "Chase and his friends got me out."

"Glad they were good for something," her father snapped. "Help me up, will ya?"

Chase rolled him to his side and sliced through the zip tie holding his wrists together. Then he held out a hand.

Alana's father stared at it, his eyes narrowed. Finally, he took Chase's hand and let him draw him to his feet. Once upright, the older man swayed.

Chase grabbed his elbow.

Alana rose and slipped an arm around his waist. Between the two of them, they steadied her father. He tried to shake free of Chase's grip.

"Give it a minute," Chase said.

"I don't need a minute." The older man swayed a little. A frown creased her father's brow, but he didn't move or try to shake free of Chase's grip again. "How did you know—"

"We got word from one of our sources that Delgado found out about you and decided to go for big money. He was going to demand ransom for Alana. If that went south, they were going to take you."

Alana's father nodded. "Since you recovered Alana, does that mean it went south for Delgado?"

"Yes, sir," Chase said. "He's on a plane to California to be turned over to the U.S. Marshals."

"Good," the older man said. "I was in the lobby when Delgado's goons came after me."

"Why didn't you stay in the room?" Alana asked.

"I was waiting to hear news about you," he said. "When they came in, the hotel staff ducked behind the counters. They tazed my bodyguard, tied him up and threatened to shoot him if I didn't go with them. Then they escorted me out the back, where you found me."

"Fortunately, we were just pulling into the hotel when we heard Delgado had sent his second in command to take you." Alana leaned her cheek against her father's arm. "Thank God we got here when we did."

Her father nodded and smoothed his over his damaged clothes. "Yes, your timing was impeccable." He looked over her shoulder.

Chase had taken a step back, giving her father all the room he needed to reunite with his daughter and giving him time to be a father.

Alana's heart swelled. The man was insightful, honorable and protective.

HER FATHER WATCHED him as well.

Hank and Chase checked the two downed cartel members for pulses. Finding both alive, they applied pressure to their wounds until an ambulance could arrive.

Ten minutes later, the Mexican police and two ambulances arrived amid flashing lights and wailing sirens. Four police units pulled in, surrounding the loading dock.

Chase, Trevor, Gina and Hank had

grounded their rifles. Hank and Chase waited for the medical technicians to take over before they straightened and joined Gina and Trevor, where they stood with Alana, holding their hands in the air as the police surrounded them.

The hotel manager emerged onto the loading dock and spoke in Spanish to the officer in charge.

When the officer in charge turned to Chase, he answered all questions in a straightforward, patient manner, his bearing and tone something Alana recognized in all of his team. They were men of authority without the need for volume or aggression. When a younger officer got snippy with him, Chase didn't let it affect him. He answered in an easy, non-threatening way.

Hank's men emerged from the tree line, escorting the injured man and the guy who'd tried to drive away. The uninjured man's wrists were zip-tied behind his back. The other had his uninjured wrist zip-tied to his partner's zip-tie.

The officer in charge studied the faces of the four cartel members, and his eyes narrowed. He nodded his head slightly, as if he recognized some, if not all four.

Chase, Trevor and Hank gave their statements about the incident at the hotel only. Hank told them they were trained to protect and extract hostages. He gave the officer the name of his contact in the Mexican government, who could vouch for his team and their permission to bear arms in Mexico.

The officer stepped away, placed a call and came back minutes later to let them know they were free to go. The police would hand over the cartel members to federal officers.

All through the investigation, Alana's father watched Chase. "He handles himself well," her father commented.

"He does," Alana said with an inordinate amount of pride. "He doesn't get rattled easily."

"He came for me first," her father admitted quietly as if admitting it was hard for him. "He stepped out into the open to help me, placing himself in the line of fire." He drew in a deep breath and released it slowly. "He didn't have to do that."

Alana nodded. "It's what he is. A protector."

"As soon as he pulled the hood off, he checked for my pulse like it was instinct."

She smiled. "It probably was. He was a Navy SEAL. He spent his time in service making sure his people came back alive. He entered Delgado's compound with just three other people to rescue me. Outnumbered at least ten to one. Hank was on his way, but Chase wasn't waiting for him. I don't know if I would've survived had he waited."

Her father grunted. Not a response to her words, but not disparaging, either. Progress?

Once the police were done with the men of the Brotherhood Protectors, they left.

Chase stepped in front of Alana and her father. "Are we all good?"

Alana nodded.

Her father held out his hand. "My daughter tells me that you went into Delgado's compound to rescue her."

"Yes, sir." Chase gripped the man's hand. "Three others and I, until Hank and his team arrived."

Alana's father gripped Chase's hand for a long moment, his eyes strangely glassy. "I owe you a debt I can never repay."

Chase shook his head. "You owe me nothing. I'd have gone in no matter what. Alana's my wife."

"She's my daughter. My only child," her father said, his words gruff. He released

Chase's hand, his brow furrowing. "I'm not a man who apologizes easily or often." He met Chase's gaze and lifted his bruised chin. "I was wrong about you. Wrong about the situation I walked into. You're obviously not a gold-digger. A gold-digger would've sent someone else in to rescue my daughter. He wouldn't have risked his life for her. Your actions aren't those of a man who married my daughter for money. I can be obstinate and hard-headed."

"I've noticed," Chase said, the corner of his mouth twitched.

Alana's father's eyes narrowed for a moment, then he surprised her when he burst out laughing.

Apparently, it surprised Chase as well.

"You don't miss much, do you?" her father said.

"I try to be aware," Chase said.

Her father looked from Alana to Chase and back. "You'll take care of her, won't you?"

"Yes, sir," Chase said. "Every single day. And she'll let me know when I'm doing it wrong." He winked at Alana, making her heart flutter.

"Oh, she will, all right." Her father glanced her way with a tenderness he hadn't shown her since she was much younger. "She gets that from her mother."

Alana's eyes filled with tears as she hugged her father. "I love you, Daddy."

"I love you, too, sweetheart," he said into her hair. "I only want you safe and happy. This man proved he can keep you safe. If he makes you happy, I won't stand in your way."

THEY MOVED INTO THE HOTEL, where the manager arranged for them all to have a late dinner and drinks.

Chase sat on one side of Alana through the meal while her father sat on the other. Like Mr. Neal, he didn't want her out of his sight, not after almost losing her. This woman, whom he'd married in a drunken stupor, had found her way under his skin. Strong, courageous and feisty, she was everything he could have ever wanted in a wife and hadn't known he needed.

After the meal, the team dispersed. Gina went with Carson, Alana's father retired to a room the manager had arranged for him, and the others convened in the bar.

Chase took Alana's hand. "Want to go for a walk?"

She nodded. "I haven't had a chance to walk on the beach in the moonlight," She laughed. "At least not that I remember."

They walked down to the beach but didn't go far before they sat and stared out at the star-filled night.

For a long time, neither said anything.

Chase opened his mouth several times, wanting to find out where she stood on their marriage. He closed his mouth before uttering any words, afraid that if he asked, she'd say she wanted to end their marriage.

"We haven't discussed the annulment," Alana said softly, breaking the silence.

His pulse picked up as he stared out at a calm ocean. "No, we haven't."

Gentle waves lapped at the shore, the sound soothing when his heart was racing.

"I don't want one," she said.

Chase let go of the breath he hadn't realized he'd been holding. "Good." Joy swelled in his chest, making it impossible for him to say more in that moment.

"Good?" She looked across at him, an eyebrow cocked. "Is that all you've got?"

"It's the best news I've heard all night." He pulled her into his arms. "I don't want an annulment either. I believe that, in our inebriated state, we let our walls down and were open to something we might've missed had we met when we were sober."

She smiled up at him. "Best tequila shots I ever drank," she whispered and lifted her lips to his. "No regrets."

"No regrets," he echoed against her mouth as he took her lips and gave her his heart.

EPILOGUE

Two weeks later

After a week in Cabo San Lucas and another in Eagle Rock, Montana, Alana and Chase flew to San Diego to wrap up Chase's life there.

After a day filled with cleaning and sorting through the contents of Chase's apartment, they'd ended the day with Alana sitting on a stool in McP's Irish Pub in Coronado, California. She smiled as she watched her hunky former Navy SEAL walk across the floor toward her, a grin spreading across his face. When he reached her, he gathered her into his arms and planted a kiss full on her lips, a kiss she gave back as good as she got.

A full minute and a half later, and to the

wolf calls of the men around him, Chase lifted his head.

Alana's cheeks heated, and she chuckled, pulling away just enough to look up into his eyes. "What took you so long?"

"I had to drive around the parking lot several times before I could find a parking space." He kissed the tip of her nose. "Did you miss me?"

She nodded. "I did. Why were you grinning so much?"

"It's my natural reaction to seeing my wife," Chase said, the grin broadening. "I can't help but think how lucky I am that you chose me."

"I thought *you* chose *me*, and I just went along with it because I had nothing better to do in Cabo San Lucas," she teased him.

"You mean you haven't since fallen for me because of my skills in a kayak?"

"Uh, no," she said. "You flipped it and took me down with you. You nearly drowned me. If it had been in Cabo, I wouldn't have minded as much. But getting dunked in a glacier-fed stream in Montana wasn't my idea of a good time."

"Hmm. That's not how I remembered it. I thought I saved you from drowning after you capsized us while trying to kiss me." He nibbled a line along the length of her neck, slowing to test the pulse beating at the base. "Either way, we lived, and we're here now," he murmured against her skin.

"Why did you bring me here? I thought we were going to stay Montana, where you'll be working now."

"I had a couple of things to take care of first. You know, pack my apartment and forward my mail. And I wanted you to meet my family—the brothers who've meant the most to me for the past few years. They've been my unit, my team and my family. Despite how bad they smell, I'm going to miss the bastards. Besides, I wanted to see their faces when they hear what we've done. They aren't going to believe it when I tell them." He turned her toward the group of men gathered around a large table.

"This is your family?" Alana held back a frown pulling at her forehead. "You didn't tell me we were meeting a big group of people."

"I didn't want this motley crew to scare you away before you got to know them." Chase gave a sharp whistle to get their attention. "Hey, you bunch of dirtbags, I want you to meet Alana."

"Alana!" As one, all of the men lifted their drinks and shouted her name.

"Because you're all family to me, I wanted you to be here to get to know someone I care a great deal about. This is Mrs. Alana Neal Flannigan, my wife."

"What? You're kidding!" one yelled.

"Well, I'll be damned," said another.

Yet a third man slapped his leg and laughed. "The most confirmed bachelor took the plunge. That doesn't bode well for the rest of us."

"Let me introduce you to them by their favorite drinks—which we use as our 'handles' on the team." He pointed to the first man to his right, a dark-haired man with soulful brown eyes. "This is Dirty Martini, or Dirtman for short. He doesn't talk much, well, except to cuss. You'll get used to him."

Dirty Martini shot Chase his middle finger and gave Alana a chin lift of recognition.

Chase pointed to a man with a high-and-tight haircut, wearing a crisp white button-down shirt and a navy-blue blazer. "That's Bourbon Neat. He likes the expensive stuff."

Alana smiled at the man and shook his hand. He dressed like a man on his way to a business meeting, except relaxed like being so cool was as natural as breathing.

Pointing to a man sipping from a wine goblet, Chase said, "This is Red Wine. He likes to think he's sophisticated."

The man in question tossed a pretzel at Chase. "Nah, I just never developed a taste for beer. Why suffer drinking piss water, when I can have a smooth, red wine?" He lifted his glass to Alana. "Welcome to the family, sister."

"Cold Beer likes his beer cold and his women hot." Chase tipped his head toward a man holding a frosty beer mug. "He can flip a beer cap into any can. He's won money from that particular skill."

"Damn right." The man with the neatly trimmed beard lifted his mug in salute. "Still can't believe Salty Dog got hitched. You must be some special kind of woman. Congrats."

"She is the best kind of woman," Chase said and pointed to a man with a glass containing a dark liquid. "Single Malt's not as pretentious as his choice of liquor would lead you to believe. He just doesn't drink if single malt isn't available. He's acquired a taste for the good shit."

Single Malt nodded. "I don't settle for less than what I want."

"Stick with your standards, man," Chase said and turned to a man with a mixed drink. "Rusty Nail likes the hard stuff because he's a hard case."

Rusty Nail lifted his glass. "Don't listen to him. I like my liquor hard, and my women soft. I'm a teddy bear at heart."

"Last but not least is our permanent designated driver, Black Coffee." Chase indicated a man with dark hair, sipping a steaming mug of java. "We're fortunate to have him stone sober, for the most part. Although on occasion, he likes to mix a little Irish cream in his mug."

Black Coffee nodded his head. "Glad to oblige. Nice to meet you, Alana."

Chase continued. "And you know Sex on the Beach, who earned his moniker by being the biggest womanizer of the lot."

Carson, wearing a shirt with palm trees and hula girls, grinned. "That's right. Two of my favorite things. Sex and beaches."

Alana laughed. "Thank goodness, some people can be reformed."

"Some of these guys need it," Chase said.

The men threw cardboard coasters at him.

"Some of us don't want to be reformed," said the one Chase had called Dirty Martini.

"By the way, what did you do with Delgado?" she asked Carson.

Carson grinned. "That's classified."

Alana snorted. "Classified, my ass." But she shook her head. "One of these days you'll have to tell us."

"One of these days, I might," Carson said.

Alana grinned and looked up to Chase. "Your team has some interesting names. And that's where you got the nickname Salty Dog?" she asked. "You like grapefruit juice and vodka?"

He nodded. "Yes, it is. Now that my rowdy family is here, and because my girl has a propensity for forgetting some of the most important moments of her life, I wanted you all to bear witness to what I'm about to do."

Alana frowned. "What's this all about?" Her heart fluttered in her chest, and butterflies erupted in her belly.

Chase puffed out his chest and dug a hand into the pocket of his jeans as he pulled out a small box and sank to one knee.

His friends whistled, hooted and called out.

"Go, Salty Dog!" Rusty Nail called out.

"Do it right, old man!" Carson yelled.

Dirty Martini snorted. "Another one bites the dust."

Chase shot them a glaring look. "Shut up and listen. I need witnesses."

Every one of the men pulled out their cell phones and hit their video recording buttons.

Alana's knees weakened as she stared down at Chase looking up at her.

"Just so you know," he said. "I've cleared this with your father."

Her breath caught. "My father? You two are talking?"

Chase nodded. "Yes, we are. He doesn't hate me anymore."

She chuckled. "You're a miracle worker. My father hates everyone."

"Not his son-in-law. Not anymore. We've bonded. And I worked it out with Hank Patterson that I'd go to work with the Hawaii branch of the Brotherhood Protectors. It helps that Jace Hawkins and I worked together for a couple of years. He put in a good word for me with Patterson."

His gaze settled on her expression. His wife's eyes were beginning to look a little glassy. His wife. Man, he liked the sound of it.

"Are you kidding me?" Alana's eyes widened

and she flung her arms around his neck. "You're going to work in Hawaii?"

Chase frowned. "I thought you'd like to be close to home—and your dad was all for it. For the record, he doesn't expect you to go back to work for him, unless you want to."

She leaned back, her brow dipping low on her forehead. "I thought you had your heart set on Montana?"

"If you want to go to Montana, Hank left that option open as well. Or we can go to the Louisiana bayou or Colorado."

She laughed. "I love where I'm from. Hawaii is in my blood and bones. Of course, I'd love to stay there, and it would be nice to be close to my father, as cantankerous as he can be. I know all the Brotherhood Protectors there. They helped me when my friend Kimo and I were kidnapped. Hawk is an amazing man. You'll love the entire team. Which means more family and friends."

She'd already filled him in on her last adventure, so he didn't wince too hard at the mention of it. "Good. Hawaii, it is. But that's not all." Chase took a deep breath and launched. "Alana Neal Flannigan, you've shown me that marriage isn't as scary as I always thought. You've shown me how strong a woman can be, and how much joy she can bring to a relationship. I wanted to show you how much that has meant to me by giving you a token of my love." He opened the box and extracted a beautiful ring with a large diamond solitaire at the center, the band lined with smaller diamonds. "I know we skipped the whole engagement thing. So, we don't have to do that. And we got married before we got to know each other, and I have the certificate to prove it. So, Alana, will you *not* annul our marriage, will you stay married to me for richer or poorer, until death do us part?" He took her left hand in his and held it with the ring poised to join the wedding band on her ring finger. He paused, waiting for her response.

The lump forming in Alana's throat almost made it impossible for her to answer. She swallowed several times, delaying the inevitable conclusion.

"Oh, sweetheart," Chase said. "Don't hesitate. You're getting me worried."

She laughed, the joy of the moment bringing tears to her eyes. Finally, she forced words past her vocal cords. "Yes, yes, yes," she said, and pulled him to his feet and into her arms. "I wasn't sure who you were at first, but you've shown me a man I can trust to save me when the cartel is after me. A man who likes to dance and isn't afraid to do it in front of every barhopping drunk in Cabo San Lucas. And you've shown me that falling in love doesn't have to take months to get there. When you find the right person, you just know, even through a haze of alcohol. I love you, Chase Flannigan…my best friend, my hero and my husband. I'll stay married to you for as long as we both shall live."

Alana flung her arms around her husband's neck and kissed him with all the love and passion she felt for the stranger she'd woken up married to in a foreign country.

The men congratulated Chase amid hugs and good-natured ribbing. All of them lined up to kiss Alana's cheek before they resumed their seats and lifted their drinks for a toast.

"To the newlyweds!" Carson said. "May they live long and procreate. We need the next generation of Navy SEALs to carry on the tradition."

A cheer went up from the table of Navy

SEALs, and the party of Alana's life began in earnest.

THE END

I hope you enjoyed Alana's Hero. This story was previously published as Hot SEAL Salty Dog but has been revised and expanded with additional scenes to bring it into the Brotherhood Protectors Hawaii series. If you want to read more about Chase's former teammates check out the SEALS in Paradise series. If you want to learn more about Alana's previous kidnapping, read Kimo's Hero. As always, thank you for reading the Brotherhood Protectors books.

Keep reading for the first chapter of
ROGUE
a Stealth Operations Specialists book.

ROGUE

STEALTH OPERATIONS
SPECIALISTS BOOK #2

New York Times & USA Today
Bestselling Author

ELLE JAMES

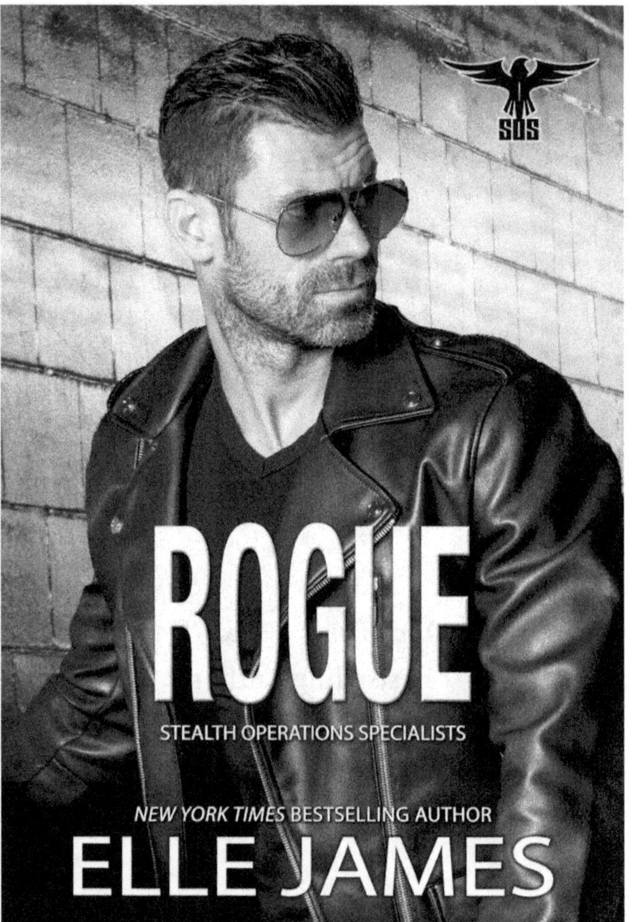

SOS

ROGUE

STEALTH OPERATIONS SPECIALISTS

NEW YORK TIMES BESTSELLING AUTHOR

ELLE JAMES

PROLOGUE

THREE WEEKS AGO, 11:47 pm...

SHE STEPPED out of the service elevator, wearing black, head-to-toe, face obscured, gloves, silent shoes, a black knife strapped to her thigh. Nothing shiny. No noise. A shadow moving along the corridor of the luxury Dallas penthouse apartment. She was Onyx. In her element.

At the apartment entrance, she worked the security device, entering the code she'd been given. Once inside, she disarmed the device and killed the surveillance cameras.

As she moved through the apartment, she went through her mental checklist.

Disable security – check

Target: Senator Richard Morales

Location: Master bedroom, northeast corner

Weapon: No noise. Close contact. Knife

Exit: Service elevator, twelve seconds from target room

Moving quickly and efficiently through the living room with floor-to-ceiling windows overlooking the Dallas skyline, the glow of the city lighting her way. She passed family photos propped on a sofa table behind a pristine white leather couch. Photos of a beautiful wife with long blond hair, smiling at the camera. Another of two teenage daughters, both dark-haired, wearing white, flowing dresses and sandals, taken at sunset on the beach.

She moved past them into the kitchen and beyond, pushing the images to the back of her mind, closing them off as she replayed her handler's words, given during her mission briefing.

"Morales is selling government secrets to the Russians," Viktor Rousseau had said in his deep, intense tone. "He's a traitor. Eliminating him will stop the flow of secrets, thus protecting our country. Without you, the

Russians will use the information he supplies to target our weaknesses, dismantle our defenses and destroy our country. You must save our country."

Her mission: eliminate the traitor, save the country

When she reached the door to the master bedroom, a shaft of light spilled out through the crack. A voice sounded from within.

"Strickland and his threats can go to hell. I'm going public with the Kaufman contracts tomorrow. He can't get away with this. He needs to be stopped. The American people deserve to know."

She froze. Strickland? Was he talking about Deputy Director Alan Strickland? The man who signed off on her missions? A knot formed in the pit of her belly. Viktor trusted him. Took orders from him. *She'd* taken orders from him.

She stood paralyzed for seconds—an eternity for an Onyx operative.

Ignore the static. Viktor's voice echoed in her head. *Complete the mission.*

Morales's voice cut through the words in her thoughts. "Strickland is using government black ops funds to build a private army."

Morales paused. "This is no joke. I have proof. He's using them to take out his opposition, clearing a path for Kaufman and his illegal contracts."

That knot in her gut spoke to her. *This is wrong.*

Instinct she'd buried for years, the instinct that had kept her alive on the streets of Dallas, kicked in.

She backed away from the door and moved swiftly through the penthouse. As she passed through the kitchen, she fished an SD disk from her pocket.

"I can't do this anymore." She laid the disk on the white quartz countertop. If the private army Strickland was building consisted of her and the others in the Onyx program, the senator would need what was on the disk to add to whatever proof he had.

The disk contained information she wasn't supposed to have. Information about the Onyx program. Until she'd overheard the senator's words, she hadn't realized what it was really about.

A private army?

Had Strickland used her and the others in a

sick plan to remove his opposition? Had the people he'd had them target been innocent?

Her stomach roiled.

They'd been trained, groomed and manipulated to believe whatever Viktor or Strickland told them. They'd believed they were helping their country, that what they were doing was right. That they were the good guys, taking out bad people.

She eased through the penthouse door, closing it quietly behind her. Head down, she hurried for the service elevator and counted the seconds it took to get her to the ground floor. Once the door opened, she slipped out the back of the building, through the door she'd rigged to disable the security. Hugging the side of the building, she moved in the shadows past the loading dock and crossed quickly to hide behind the giant trash bins.

A linen-cleaning service truck approached the loading dock and backed in, headlights shining on the trash bins.

She closed one eye to keep from losing all her night vision.

Finally, the driver turned off the truck and the lights.

With both eyes open, the one still adjusting, she thought she saw a shadow slip around the side of the loading dock and into the building. She couldn't be certain with her eyes still correcting after being blinded by the truck's headlights.

The driver climbed down from his truck and up onto the dock.

She made her move, floating through the night like a ghost, moving from shadow to shadow until she was a few blocks from the high-rise apartment building. Pulling her communications devices from her ears, she dropped them on the pavement and smashed them with her heel, severing contact with Viktor. With her life.

Walking away from a mission, refusing to complete a job, was a death sentence. She'd gone from being an asset to becoming a liability. A loose end.

A target.

In a matter of seconds, she'd turned her world upside down. She needed time to think about her next moves in a safe place. A place only she knew about.

Because of the work she'd done for Onyx, she'd cultivated several safehouses she could use when things got hot, and she needed a place to chill and lay low for a while.

Moving swiftly, she made her way through the city, clinging to shadows, always looking over her shoulder.

Nobody walked away from Onyx.

Anyone who dared to leave the organization was carried out, and the body was buried where no one would find it.

ANOTHER SHADOW SLIPPED through the night, triggering the motion sensor of the exterior surveillance camera on the apartment building. A figure dressed in black entered the high-rise and took the service elevator up to the penthouse.

Entering the apartment was easy since the security alarm had previously been disarmed.

No one heard the intruder or the shot fired from a handgun fitted with a silencer. On the way out, a shadowy trespasser moved back through the apartment, pausing at the white quartz kitchen counter. The SD disc was swapped for a different calling card.

A stone.

Black onyx.

. . .

SEVENTY-TWO HOURS LATER...

"YOU ARE ONYX," Viktor's deep voice drilled into her.

"No," she cried, unable to move or free herself from the bonds holding her. "I'm Keira."

Keira Davies jerked awake, gasping for air and struggling to free herself of the bindings trapping her arms and legs, only to realize the ties that bound her weren't ties at all. She kicked her way out of a sleeping bag she'd staged in yet another one of her safehouses—this one being a rarely used warehouse on the outskirts of Waco, instead of the house in the suburbs of Dallas or the cabin in the piney woods near Tyler.

Three days on the run. Three different safehouses. And she had a feeling, if not visual confirmation, that someone was getting close to catching up to her.

She stood, stretched and switched on a light in the office where she'd set up camp. Spread across a desktop lay photos taken from surveillance cameras, more photos she'd taken herself over the past months. For some time, she'd been following the Kaufman Syndicate and its leader, Marcus Kaufman. Some of the photos were of him. Others were of the people with whom he was closely connected or with whom he conducted business.

Among those photos were some of her mentor, Viktor Rousseau; Deputy Director Alan Strickland; Marcus Kaufman; his girl-friend, Layne Jenner; and Senator Richard Morales. She'd laid some out across the desk, taped some to the wall and connected the photos with strips of string between those she'd seen together. All the work she'd done gathering intel had been for the sole purpose of digging deeper into the organization that had trained her to do their bidding under the pretext of helping her country.

Keira fired up her laptop, tuning in to the latest news from Dallas.

A male anchorman, with intense dark eyes, stared into the camera. "Investigators are still searching for the person responsible for the murder of Senator Richard Morales in his penthouse apartment. Anyone with information about the shooting should notify the police."

The television station aired a shadowy image of a person dressed all in black slipping into the apartment building, captured by a surveillance camera.

"If you know or recognize this person of interest, notify the police. There is a one-hundred-thousand-dollar reward posted for information leading to the arrest and conviction of the one responsible for the senator's death. So far, all the police have to go on is the video and a black onyx stone left on the kitchen counter in the senator's apartment."

Keira's hand shook as she closed the lid of her laptop. A combination of dread and rage flooded her thoughts. The perp's clothing, the way he'd entered and left the apartment complex and the signature black onyx stone were hallmarks of the work of Onyx.

Just not this Onyx operative. Who would know the difference? She had been sent to do the job. She had been part of the Onyx collective. Part of the organization, as Morales had put it, was being recruited and trained to provide Strickland a private army to eliminate his opposition.

Keira refused to be manipulated and coerced into doing their dirty work anymore. To keep Strickland and his cronies from continuing to play God by brainwashing young women and girls, she'd have to collect enough information to nail the bastards.

On the wall over the desk, she'd tacked photos of the key players, the locations and the connections she'd been gathering for months before the senator's murder.

"You trained us to be invisible. To trust what you told us as truth. To trust the mission."

Keira shook her head and cursed as she stared at the faces on the wall.

It was all a lie.

Now, they'd sent in the clean-up crew to set her up to take the fall for Morales's death.

Her burner phone chirped. The sound, suddenly breaking the complete silence, made her jump.

Keira stared down at the text message sent from an Unknown caller.

They're coming for you. Move now—Your friend

Instinct kicked in. With less than ninety seconds to react, she dove into action.

Keira grabbed the jug of accelerant, doused

the wall, the desk and the floor. She set the timer on the detonator, shoved it into a lump of plastic explosives, grabbed her pre-packed go-bag and tucked the burner phone into her pocket. Rather than go down and out, she pulled her hoodie up over her head, slung the go-bag strap across her body, then climbed the twenty rungs of a metal ladder and exited through the maintenance door to the rooftop.

Fifteen steps to the edge of the roof. An eight-foot drop to the rooftop of the adjoining building. With her bag slung behind her, Keira leaped from the safehouse roof to the neighboring roof. When her shoes hit, she tucked her arms against her sides and let her knees bend to absorb the impact. A moment later, she rolled on her side and came back up on her feet. Twelve strides running across the roof as she'd practiced half a dozen times. On the far side, she'd find the exterior metal ladder that was retracted when not in use but could be easily extended to reach all the way to the ground. She slung her leg over and started down the ladder. When she reached the next section, she flipped a lever and released the extension. It slid downward, stopping two feet above the ground. Keira hurried the rest of the way down and jumped free when she had only four feet remaining.

Keira shot a quick glance at her watch. Eighty-five seconds. Five seconds faster than before. Two minutes now until show time. She slipped across the street and found a shadowy position in an alley behind a large trash bin and waited, her gaze trained on the building she'd vacated. As she waited, she wondered who was behind the text message warning her to get out. As far as she knew, she had no friends. Refusing to perform her given mission, she'd cut all ties with her trainer and other trainees. She was truly on her own.

After a minute passed, Keira wondered if she'd been fed a false alarm.

At that moment, a sleek black SUV charged down the street, coming to a hard stop in front of the warehouse. Four men in tactical gear climbed out of the SUV. Not police. Not federal.

Two more dark SUVs skidded to a halt behind the first, adding eight more men to the team gathering in front of the warehouse. A fourth black SUV arrived.

Her breath caught, and her jaw hardened when she recognized the two men who emerged.

Marcus Kaufman and her mentor, Viktor Rousseau.

Viktor stepped into the middle of the team of mercenaries.

Though she couldn't hear his words clearly, she could read Viktor's lips as he told the men, *Find her. She must not leave Texas alive.*

Armed with military-grade rifles, the men in combat gear ran toward the warehouse. They used a crowbar to pry open the door and rushed in.

Viktor joined Kaufman and spoke a few words Keira couldn't hear. They were standing too close with their heads averted for her to lip-read either.

Marcus nodded once, his eyes narrowed at the building.

Using her cell phone, she zoomed in and snapped a photo of the men at the exact moment Marcus turned away.

The two men climbed into the SUV.

Twenty seconds...

Ten... Nine... Eight... Seven... Six... Five... Four

The vehicle containing Marcus and Viktor drove away from the warehouse.

Keira drew in a breath. Held it.

Three... Two...

She ducked behind the heavy metal bin, covered her ears and closed her eyes.

Boom!

The explosion rocked the ground beneath her, but the trash bin shielded her from flying debris.

Flames rose and quickly consumed what remained of the warehouse, turning the cloud of dust into an impenetrable orange fog filling the night.

Keira rose from behind the trash bin and hurried away from the scene. Several blocks away, she emerged from the choking dust and smoke, climbed onto the motorcycle she'd stashed in an alley and drove away.

Adrenaline still racing through her system, she headed south, taking the backroads, putting as much distance between herself and the people who wanted her dead.

If not for the warning, she might not have made it out of the warehouse in time.

Who had warned her? Who knew about her safehouses? How had they found her?

This time had been close. Too close.

Would she be as lucky next time?

Anger spurred her on.

For the past ten years, she'd been groomed, trained and molded into Onyx. She'd learned to be invisible, to blend into the shadows. A ghost. A lethal weapon. It had been her identity.

Before Onyx, she'd been nothing. Homeless. Living on the streets of Dallas. Barely surviving. As part of Onyx, she'd had a purpose. Or so she'd thought. Their brainwashing and manipulation had been all too complete. Too effective. She'd been Onyx.

Now, she had to relearn who she was. Who Keira Davies was. Plus, gather enough evidence to put the people away who'd made her a weapon to be feared, before they erased her completely.

TRUCKSTOP on the outskirts of Austin, 8:30 am

Keira entered the shower stall in the truck stop, carrying the supplies she'd purchased at a drug store several blocks away. She stripped out of the hoodie she'd worn since leaving

Waco and stuffed it into the trash receptacle. She stripped out of the rest of her clothes and hung them on a hook, out of the way. She pulled on the pair of latex gloves that had come with the kit and went to work.

Following the directions on the box, she applied chemicals that would bleach the color out of her naturally dark brown hair. When she'd waited the recommended time, she stood beneath the shower and rinsed the chemicals from her hair, then patted it dry with one of the towels she'd purchased. Then she applied the toner and waited twenty minutes. She rinsed the toner out of her hair, squirted conditioner into her palm, rubbed it into her hair and rinsed again. She finished her shower, washing her entire body with body wash, glad to be clean after running for over three days.

After she dried off, she bent over and brushed her hair toward the floor. Tangles removed, she grabbed the length in a loose ponytail near the crown of her head. With the scissors she'd purchased, she hacked off the ponytail four inches from her scalp.

When she straightened, her hair fell in damp layers almost to her shoulders. When it dried, curls would make it appear shorter and frame her face, helping to hide some of her features.

Keira dressed quickly, the hair color and cut having taken too long already. She'd been in the shower stall for over an hour. Truck stops had security systems. Systems accessible via the internet. If one of the cameras had caught her face beneath the hoodie, it might only be a matter of time before facial recognition software found her, and before Onyx and Kaufman Syndicate located her and sent their goons to eliminate the threat.

She'd ditched her dark jeans for the faded blue jeans she'd picked up in a thrift store. A long-sleeve chambray shirt tied at the waist and worn dingo boots would help transform her from black ops to farmhand. Believable at a truck stop in Texas. The battered straw she had pulled out of her go-bag would hide her eyes and complete her disguise, for the moment. She had a backup wig, baseball caps, different-colored shirts and lightweight jackets she could throw on at a moment's notice. The go-bag was reversible, allowing her to change the color and carry it as a duffel bag or wear it as a backpack.

Disappearing and blending into a crowd were all part of her Onyx training. She just had to make sure she used it well enough to fool her mentors and other operatives.

Keira stepped out of the shower stall and checked her reflection in a mirror. She didn't recognize herself from the woman who'd walked in an hour ago. But she recognized the desperate street rat from ten years earlier—the girl who had been dragged into the police station and handed over to a social worker.

"There's this program I know of. One that can help you get off the street. Learn new skills. Give you training and purpose," the woman had said. That woman had been Layne Jenner. How had she flown under the radar for so long, disguised as a social worker? What state official had rubber-stamped her background check?

Yeah, Keira had chosen the "program" over foster homes where the foster "parents" were in it for the money and couldn't care less about the kids and teens for whom they were supposed to provide a loving, stable home. She and her sister, Kit, had been in a few. They'd carried their garbage bag of meager belongings that were eventually lost or replaced with worn hand-me-downs. She'd stuck it out for Kit until they'd ended up in a home where the foster parents' oldest son raped Keira. When he went after Kit, Keira had nearly beaten the teen to death with a baseball bat. She'd taken Kit and run away, going from a bad situation to worse.

At sixteen and eight years old, sleeping under a bridge, they'd been captured by a pimp who'd sold them into a sex trafficking ring where they'd been drugged into submission.

In Kit's case, she'd been drugged to death.

The morning Keira had woken in the filthy room where they'd locked up at night to find Kit lying cold and still beside her, she'd lost her shit.

She'd begged them to kill her, too. When they wouldn't, she'd tried to hang herself with her clothes. They'd taken away her clothing and fed her food laced with drugs.

Keira had stopped eating for a couple of days, giving her portions to the other girls in the room. By then, the drugs had worn off. For the first time since her capture, she'd been able to think clearly enough to plot her escape. Pretending she was drugged too much to be a threat, she'd waited until one of the men carried her out of her cell and tossed her in a van. Thinking she was out cold, they'd ignored her. At a stop in downtown Dallas, when they'd gotten out to chat with someone, she'd eased open the door, slipped out, then run naked and barefoot through the streets. Stopping at a donation box, she'd scavenged jeans and a shirt. She'd even found a pair of ratty tennis shoes. Though they were too big, she'd managed to tie what was left of the laces tight enough they wouldn't fall off if she ran. As the sun rose in the city, she found an alley where a giant trash bin overflowed and an old mattress had been discarded. It was there she'd passed out from exhaustion.

It was also there that the police had found her, dragged her into the police station and turned her over to social worker, Layne Jenner. Keira had lost everything she'd ever cared about. Her parents when she was only twelve. Her sister. Her will to live. All she'd had left was anger. Deep burning anger. At life. At "the system." At men who did whatever they wanted because she couldn't fight back. At herself, for Kit's death.

When Keira entered the training compound of Onyx, Viktor had been there to greet her. A big, hulk of a man with a shiny bald head and tattoos covering much of his body. He'd laid one of his meaty hands on her shoulder.

Keira had flinched, ready for another man to slam a fist in her face or gut. She'd learned that was what they did. Why would he be different?

Instead, he'd stared straight into her eyes and said, "Keira, from now on, you're not a victim. You're a weapon. Weapons don't feel."

All of those memories rushed over her as she stared at the blond stranger in the mirror. For all those years, she'd locked her feelings away, refusing to think about her little sister or the life they'd had before her parents had died in a car wreck. For a little longer, she would keep those emotions tamped down. Long enough to bring down the people who'd fed her lies and made her think she was doing good. They'd made her think that she belonged. Her jaw hardened, and her dark eyes narrowed.

"I'm not a weapon. I'm not Onyx," she whispered through clenched teeth. She placed the straw cowboy hat on her head. "I'm Keira Davies, and I'm about to make a lot of powerful people very sorry they screwed with me." She slung her go-bag over her shoulder and lifted her chin. "I'm done with being used."

If you enjoyed this excerpt of
ROGUE
read the rest of the story
ROGUE

ELLE JAMES also writing as MYLA JACKSON is a *New York Times* and *USA Today* Bestselling author of books including cowboys, intrigues and paranormal adventures that keep her readers on the edges of their seats. When she's not at her computer, she's traveling, snow skiing, boating, or riding her ATV, dreaming up new stories. Learn more about Elle James at www.ellejames.com

Website | Facebook | Twitter | GoodReads | Newsletter | BookBub | Amazon

Or visit her alter ego Myla Jackson at mylajackson.com
Website | Facebook | Twitter | Newsletter

Follow Me!
www.ellejames.com
ellejamesauthor@gmail.com

Stealth Operations Specialists Series

Saint Nick (#1)

Rogue (#2)

Crusher (#3)

Draco (#4)

A Killer Series

Chilled (#1)

Scorched (#2)

Erased (#3)

Brotherhood Protectors International

Athens Affair (#1)

Belgian Betrayal (#2)

Croatia Collateral (#3)

Dublin Debacle (#4)

Edinburgh Escape (#5)

France Face-Off (#6)

Brotherhood Protectors Hawaii

Kalea's Hero (#1)

Leilani's Hero (#2)

Kiana's Hero (#3)

Casey's Hero (#4)

Maliea's Hero (#5)

Emi's Hero (#6)

Sachie's Hero (#7)

Kimo's Hero (#8)

Alana's Hero (#9)

Bayou Brotherhood Protectors

Remy (#1)

Gerard (#2)

Lucas (#3)

Beau (#4)

Rafael (#5)

Valentin (#6)

Landry (#7)

Simon (#8)

Maurice (#9)

Xavier (#10)

Jacques (#11)

Papa Noel (#12)

Koolaroo Ranch Series

with Kendall Talbot

Outback Secrets (#1)

Outback Escape (#2)

Outback Obsession (#3)

Outback Justice (#4)

Everglades Overwatch Series

with Jen Talty

Secrets in Calusa Cove

Pirates in Calusa Cove

Murder in Calusa Cove

Betrayal in Calusa Cove

Raven's Cliff Series

with Kris Norris

Raven's Watch (#1)

Raven's Claw (#2)

Raven's Nest (#3)

Raven's Curse (#4)

Brotherhood Protectors Yellowstone

Saving Kyla (#1)

Saving Chelsea (#2)

Saving Amanda (#3)

Saving Liliana (#4)

Saving Breely (#5)

Saving Savvie (#6)

Saving Jenna (#7)

Saving Peyton (#8)

Saving Londyn (#9)

Brotherhood Protectors Colorado

SEAL Salvation (#1)

Rocky Mountain Rescue (#2)

Ranger Redemption (#3)

Tactical Takeover (#4)

Colorado Conspiracy (#5)

Rocky Mountain Madness (#6)

Free Fall (#7)

Colorado Cold Case (#8)

Fool's Folly (#9)

Colorado Free Rein (#10)

Rocky Mountain Venom (#11)

High Country Hero (#12)

Brotherhood Protectors

Montana SEAL (#1)

Bride Protector SEAL (#2)

Montana D-Force (#3)

Cowboy D-Force (#4)

Montana Ranger (#5)

Montana Dog Soldier (#6)

Montana SEAL Daddy (#7)

Montana Ranger's Wedding Vow (#8)

Montana SEAL Undercover Daddy (#9)

Cape Cod SEAL Rescue (#10)

Montana SEAL Friendly Fire (#11)

Montana SEAL's Mail-Order Bride (#12)

SEAL Justice (#13)

Ranger Creed (#14)

Delta Force Rescue (#15)

Dog Days of Christmas (#16)

Montana Rescue (#17)

Montana Ranger Returns (#18)

Brotherhood Protectors Boxed Set 1

Brotherhood Protectors Boxed Set 2

Brotherhood Protectors Boxed Set 3

Brotherhood Protectors Boxed Set 4

Brotherhood Protectors Boxed Set 5

Brotherhood Protectors Boxed Set 6

Iron Horse Legacy

Soldier's Duty (#1)

Ranger's Baby (#2)

Marine's Promise (#3)

SEAL's Vow (#4)

Warrior's Resolve (#5)

Drake (#6)

Grimm (#7)

Murdock (#8)

Utah (#9)

Judge (#10)

Delta Force Strong

Ivy's Delta (Delta Force 3 Crossover)

Breaking Silence (#1)

Breaking Rules (#2)

Breaking Away (#3)

Breaking Free (#4)

Breaking Hearts (#5)

Breaking Ties (#6)

Breaking Point (#7)

Breaking Dawn (#8)

Breaking Promises (#9)

Hearts & Heroes Series

Wyatt's War (#1)

Mack's Witness (#2)

Ronin's Return (#3)

Sam's Surrender (#4)

Hellfire Series

Hellfire, Texas (#1)

Justice Burning (#2)

Smoldering Desire (#3)

Hellfire in High Heels (#4)

Playing With Fire (#5)

Up in Flames (#6)

Total Meltdown (#7)

Take No Prisoners Series

SEAL's Honor (#1)

SEAL'S Desire (#2)

SEAL's Embrace (#3)

SEAL's Obsession (#4)

SEAL's Proposal (#5)

SEAL's Seduction (#6)

SEAL'S Defiance (#7)

SEAL's Deception (#8)

SEAL's Deliverance (#9)

SEAL's Ultimate Challenge (#10)

Cajun Magic Mystery Series

Voodoo on the Bayou (#1)

Voodoo for Two (#2)

Deja Voodoo (#3)

Texas Billionaire Club

Tarzan & Janine (#1)

Something To Talk About (#2)

Who's Your Daddy (#3)

Love & War (#4)

Billionaire Online Dating Service

The Billionaire Husband Test (#1)

The Billionaire Cinderella Test (#2)

The Billionaire Bride Test (#3)

The Billionaire Daddy Test (#4)

The Billionaire Matchmaker Test (#5)

The Billionaire Glitch Date (#6)

The Outriders

Homicide at Whiskey Gulch (#1)

Hideout at Whiskey Gulch (#2)

Held Hostage at Whiskey Gulch (#3)

Setup at Whiskey Gulch (#4)

Missing Witness at Whiskey Gulch (#5)

Cowboy Justice at Whiskey Gulch (#6)

Boys Behaving Badly Anthologies

Rogues (#1)

Blue Collar (#2)

Pirates (#3)

Stranded (#4)

First Responder (#5)

Cowboys (#6)

Silver Soldiers (#7)

Secret Identities (#8)

Warrior's Conquest

Enslaved by the Viking Short Story

Conquests

Smokin' Hot Firemen

Protecting the Colton Bride

Protecting the Colton Bride & Colton's Cowboy Code

Heir to Murder

Secret Service Rescue

High Octane Heroes

Haunted